INCIPIENT SPECIES

Theresa Greve Løberg

Incipient Species

KOLOFON FORLAG

For my boys

Thor-Jürgen
Thor-Jakob
Petter
Kristian
Finn

For all have sinned and fall short of the glory of God.

Romans 3:23

TABLE OF CONTENTS

PART III

Prologue

Gracefully seated at a small round table in the bar, with her back tall and barely touching her chair, she took in the renovations without betraying her interest. Deciding that the mirrored wall and the dark brown paint would grow on her, the changes were to her liking. As for the upholstery, a change there was long overdue. "He is hoping to stay attuned to his clientele," she thought, appreciative of the landlord's restrained modifications. And, it being a favourite haunt of hers, a major overhaul would have been distressing. Change meted out all at once, was known to overwhelm. She was of the opinion, therefore, that in life, there was every need for constancy.

She noticed them as soon as they walked in. Headed for the bar counter, the young lady walked two paces in front of her companions and sat down on a stool while the boys slid in on either side. An air about them captured the woman's attention and, glancing at the door briefly, she reverted to the trio with intrigue. They struck her as accomplished. While picking a seat at a bar and sitting down involved very little, rarely, was this simple act performed without hesitation, nor dared she say, some awkwardness. Even on one's own in a public setting, one hesitated before sitting down. The more people there were to a party, the more hesitation there tended to be. The party of three she had just observed carried out the act with finesse. She was captivated.

Drinks arrived. Raising their glasses, she heard them say: "To the best of both worlds," as they looked into each other's eyes and took a sip of their drinks.

"Just what the doctor ordered," the woman jested in her mind, on seeing them take great delight in their drinks. She was in no doubt they were siblings. The taller boy appearing to her the eldest, she guessed the other boy and girl to be twins. Though their foreheads, noses and jawlines bore a resemblance that was unmistakable, at the same time their appearance was remarkably unique, and she marvelled to herself how enterprising nature could be.

Searching the bar's entrance for her husband once more, on not finding him there her attention returned to her strangely intriguing subjects, noting with satisfaction the perfect symmetry of their faces. In detail, commencing with the placement of their noses, whose bridges were aligned flawlessly between their rather round eyes, her gaze followed to the tips which stood midpoint above their lips. And that, she recalled resignedly, was what good looks were all about. Symmetry had much to do with beauty. But theirs was by no means a bland beauty, rather it was flawed and, therefore, the kind to captivate. The sort one was not easily bored by and she felt she would not tire of looking at them. Their mouths were quite broad, much wider than the norm. It was just as well she wasn't one to give a fig about acceptable norms.

Self-consciously, she looked in the mirror at her own middle-aged face fast losing its symmetry. Peeling away from its core, it seemed to barely hold on now. Though used to it, she was far from pleased and pinched the smile she gave her image. Where her friends had indulged in all manner of treatment, including injecting Botox, she had kept her own looks and their faces, sad to say, were now monstrosities. But it was the loss of their sense of self-preservation that concerned her the most. Botox was a known toxin, botulin! Her own image, in the new mirror the landlord hoped would draw attention to his merchandise, reflected her despair.

Observing the three young siblings again, it appeared they felt no need to converse. Their manner was relaxed, their faces bearing a disarming eagerness. Why she was sure their eyes unobtrusively searched the room, she could, therefore, not say.

As if by design, each of them appeared to scan a separate section of the room. Had she seen them discuss the manoeuvre, perhaps she would not have been perturbed, but the only words to have left their lips since coming in were those for the toast and for ordering of drinks.

"Why survey the bar?" she wondered. If they longed for excitement, she would happily inform them that, unfortunately, serenity was the rule of the day here, the very reason this was her local bar. Searching them now, she determined their manner uncontrived. They were at ease. It was all very curious. But what could it be? Could she put it down to the matter of them being related? Down to two of them being twins, perhaps? But still, she could not tell.

Considering their behaviour with interest, she declared it schooled; they were good at it! Their sophistication excited her. Suddenly, the older boy's eyes found hers and he glared. Intrigued, her upper lip lifted slightly as she experienced the stirrings of a thrill. The challenge was unmistakable: "He is warning me to stay away." But his scrutiny was fleeting, interrupted shortly after by his siblings drawing his attention to the television.

Unnerved by the encounter, she felt conflicted. "Could she be wrong?" Doubting herself in such matters was rare. Hadn't she and her colleagues perfected the behavioural science of profiling individuals who posed a threat to themselves and society at large? From a mile away, could she not spot those whose sense of self-preservation had been stripped away? And did she not train hundreds specifically for this purpose?

Flustered by her inability to see the screen and a curiosity denied, she was struggling to regain her composure. She ignored the urge to move nearer and, instead, turned in time to see her husband finally walk through the door. Hesitating before he crossed the room, he decided on the chair to her right and, realising the television screen was out of view, said, "darling, move to the bar with me, I can't watch the news from here."

"Just the encouragement I need," she thought, leading him to the space next to the siblings at the corner of the bar counter.

In view of the screen now, she saw a middle-aged man on the news talking about oil. On account of the man's glib protestations, she impulsively began to assess him. Seconds into the exercise, she took charge of herself and was persuaded to stop. After all, wasn't the news nowadays filled with middle-aged men refuting this, that or the other? Was she to spontaneously profile every one of them? Since she was retired, what would be the point?

Remembering the manner of her retirement left her mouth dry. In quick succession, she took several sips of her drink before reclining in her chair. After she had taught them all she knew, in the name of national security, the agency had taken possession of her intellectual property. Side-lined to begin with, she was later simply discarded. And now she had absolutely nothing to show for all her years of painstaking observation. Since the injustice, bitterness had gained a foothold in her life. The thought of litigation had crossed her mind, but the scales of justice could not in this instance be tipped in her favour. Any effort to rectify the injustice, would merely have added insult to injury. Besides, the cost of legal representation would have emptied her coffers.

Her husband spoke and, remembering the promise of paying each other better attention, she turned to him. Though her retirement was imposed on her, she was determined to make the most of it. They weren't off to a good start, however; ingrained habits were proving a hindrance. Television was her husband's Achilles heel, while hers, she harshly perceived, was being carried away precisely in this manner.

Unable to resist, she gave her subjects a once-over and then scrutinised their faces for a 'tell'. "What about this particular man," she wished to know, "so holds their attention?" This unabashed scrutiny in close proximity to her subjects revealed something that was not apparent before: evidence of surgically repaired cleft palates. "But in all three?" she questioned in astonishment.

The girl, with a tilt to her head and a twinkle in her eye, looked questioningly at her brothers. Their response to her silent query was a simple nod.

"Now what did *that* mean?" the woman wondered, as she turned to her husband and smiled. Without warning, her subjects stood up to leave. Straying yet again, her gaze escorted them out to the bustle of a New York City street; she could not mistake the spring in their gait. She envied them their vitality and yearned for her own. Her eyes relented when they could no longer follow, but her spirit embraced the youngsters, an impulse that baffled her. With certainty, Miranda Kitts now knew that this wasn't a case of being merely overcome by her hardwired professional instincts. "Charlie and I should move back to England," she thought, all at once feeling ill at ease.

PART I

1.   *Oak Leaf Farm*

Seeing them depart was unbearable. Listening to the tyres crunch the gravel driveway as the car gathered speed, her gaze yearningly followed. The passengers waved and she responded with enthusiasm, but when she brought her hand to her mouth, her face betrayed sadness and the kiss she blew them, was laced with regret. When they at last disappeared from sight, she frowned, her apprehension deepening. But accompanying them had proved too much for her.

Forlorn, all expression suddenly vanished from her countenance as she became oblivious to the wind that rustled its way out of the woods beyond her garden, putting a chill in the morning air and a breeze under the wings of birds going about their daily business. Even as scores alighted chirpily in the bushes next to her, she did not notice.

What if she never saw them again? What would she do then? And why was she simply expected to 'let go'? Thus preoccupied, the sun fighting its way out of the forbidding daybreak clouds escaped her; nor did she notice the fresh dew on the grass, or her flowers and shrubs glisten as the sun's freed rays struck. Anticipating the promised warmth, her plants swayed and shook the condensation off their leaves. The dahlias, with a tilt to their burdened necks, looked down on the others with a fortitude bordering on disdain. Well past its peak and emitting little scent, the lavender in the terracotta pot on the step still held firm. As always, the geraniums were mauve and happy, while the climbing roses, with the help of a trellis stood tall presiding over them all. Yet, the beauty of her garden's awakening was lost on Jane.

Thinking about other parents then, she wondered if they, at all, fretted about their children. "No, they don't, not nearly as much as I do," she murmured, biting down on her lip as she fought back tears, feeling her heart grow cold to the plight of other parents. Determining cruel the endless worrying foisted on her by motherhood, Jane wondered if she perhaps denied herself mercy. She knew the 'good book' advised against worrying. The Bible declared that worry would not add a single hour to her life. Why then did she worry, when all she had to do was look to the birds?

Perhaps she should persuade them to live at home instead. Her singular desire had always been to protect her children, to give them a safe harbour. Racking her brains further, she asked, "is there to be no mercy? No hope of redemption then?" Richard often said: "It's not normal to behave the way you do. Think about it, Jane. How is a young person to spend their youth if not pursuing their life?"

She remembered how difficult it had been when they left for university and the navy. While there, the longest visit home was two weeks. This summer, however, had been different. The children spent *every* day at home except for the last week of June, which was spent in New York. As a result, her hope had been rekindled. With her offspring under her roof, the last three months were simply glorious. Her anxiety had abated, and Richard had gladly relinquished the role of reassuring husband that he had learned to play so well. And when she imitated his typical assurance, her fondness for him caused her eyes to mist; "don't you worry about a thing Jane, they will be just *fine*."

"If only I could be assured of their safety," she thought wistfully, even though it had long been her conviction that one cannot look to 'life' for assurance. Her back grew rigid, her mind became rattled and her eyes could not see beyond her anguish. As for redemption, well, she was aware it only found its way to those who repented. Her thoughts on the matter were, however, far from the kind to gain her redemption. "No, I have *yet* to receive mercy," she thought, her every fibre screaming, "nurture and protect them. Yet nurturing and protecting them is so much harder to do when they are grown...when they have suddenly acquired a will of their own."

She recalled the words of comfort a gentleman at Benton's offered her after one of Katherine's toddler tantrums at the cash register: "Don't worry, she'll soon be over it. This stage doesn't last long; it's the older kids who keep you worrying all night long. They bring along the real problems – 'bigger children, bigger problems', that's what they say. Enjoy them while they're young," he had counselled.

Unable to see past the tantrums and the endless nights of interrupted sleep, she had not believed him. Besides what did he know? Nothing to her mind, was as debilitating. That was then, but what was she to do now? Should she take away her children's will in order to spare her nerves? More to the point, would they let her? And yet, for all her anxiety, she could not ask them outright. Especially not after the blow they had suffered in June, the smack in the face by their own President. Outrageously insolent and defiant, amid much pomp in the Rose Garden and on a patently false premise, he had pulled America out of the Paris Agreement. That came after he reversed laws enacted to prevent further pollution of the environment. After observing the President, her family had become convinced that there was no doing anything with him. To take the edge off, the children had decided to visit New York City. She had seen this a welcome diversion.

Roused from her trance by the morning chill, Jane shivered. Considering once more the empty road leading from the house and the trees that protectively flanked it, she finally noticed the finches – that neither sow nor reap – fly determinedly into the trees. Sighing, she turned to the house, stepped inside and gently closed the door behind her. Chiding herself for entertaining negative thoughts, she forced a smile. A few steps into the hallway, gathering from the silence there, she surmised: "It's going to be a long day." Ever resourceful, her next thought turned to the upcoming luncheon: "I have people to entertain tomorrow and there should be plenty to do before then."

With a sense of purpose in her stride, she walked up the stairs to her room, found a warm sweater, and slipped it on. Heading for the henhouse, she exited the house by way of the kitchen. On seeing her hens, Jane prided herself on owning a variety of breeds. The interest and robustness that the variation added to her flock pleased her. Hard at work, they pecked and searched through the sawdust that cushioned the floor. Watching their unrelenting search brought a smile to her face. She adored their pluck. "Nothing, and I mean nothing stops them," she thought captivated. Marvelling at their striking feathers, she easily understood why bird feathers had once been a favoured fashion item.

Pulling herself away, she turned her attention to the drinking cans that needed washing and refilling. On her way out, she opened a bin of seed beside the door, took a handful and lured the hens out with the seeds she threw onto the ground. She reminisced about the children feeding the hens and their delight when the hens found the pickings. If permitted, they would have fed them all day, though overfeeding was not in the hens' best interest. As much as was possible, Jane let them fend for themselves. "Let them scratch away," she said in an attempt to push all other thoughts out of her mind. Yet she strayed once again to her children, recalling a story she read to them when they were little, that of the hens losing the needle they had borrowed from the hawks, the very mishap to damn them to a never-ending search for the needle in the haystack.

"Well, today might be the day they find that needle," she laughed to herself. The busy hens did not, however, heed her laughter, abruptly ended by the memory of Alexander's innocent question: "How can the hawks be so unforgiving, Mum?"

Her silent retort had been: "Indeed, how can *nature* be so unforgiving?" and that, bearing in mind a baby in the womb. Apparently, nature had set aside just two hours for the embryo's five facial lobes to coalesce into the familiar human face we've all come to know. If somehow prevented from occurring precisely at this moment, the opportunity was lost forever.

Leaving the hens, Jane walked to the kitchen garden, her thoughts now entirely on the passengers of the car, her family. She could not comprehend her children's wish to leave once again. If saying goodbye to them was so difficult, when gone just for the day, how would she possibly cope on Monday, the day of their departure? She trembled at the thought of Peter being so far away. How often would she see him if he lived in Norway? Steadying herself she took comfort in the knowledge that Alexander and Katherine would be much closer, nearby in Norfolk, Virginia.

In the garden shed, Jane found two baskets and set off to the vegetable bed to harvest ripened tomatoes. Knowing she would be feeding thirty guests the following day she picked many more after that and harvested some onions too. Grown rather like plants in a state of nature, her crops were a great source of gratification. Pausing to rest her back, she stood up and at the furthest edge of her orchard observed autumn's grasping hand. The leaves were turning. Autumn had arrived.

"The days will again be much calmer and quieter now that the schools had reopened," she stated matter-of-factly. Since a crowded beach was no fun for her family, in days gone by, they had taken advantage and had enjoyed the beach in solitude the weekend after the labour-day holiday. Nobody would be there now. But today, they were bound for the sea. "Where are they now?" Agonising over their progress, she resolved that there was no better way to relieve anxiety than to again set eyes on the object that was the source of one's distress. Knowing her impatience, she determined, "it's better for me to stay at home where I can be of useful employment. It's better this way, really."

2. *The best of both worlds*

The passengers in the car listened to the radio. A song started to play. James Taylor. Katherine smiled and began to sing along. "In my mind, I'm gone to Carolina … " she sang, in a voice driven solely by passion and utterly lacking in melody. Alexander and Peter, her older brothers, burst out in laughter.

"Kat, stop! You know you can't sing," Peter begged.

"It doesn't mean I shouldn't sing though," she countered defiantly. "Can't you see the moonshine, gone to Carolina in my mind."

Their father, Richard, hands on the steering wheel, turned to look at Katherine who peered out the window and did not see him smile. It was a smile of affirmation. "Look at her," he thought looking in the rear-view mirror then. But Katherine beat him to it and when their eyes met, she broadly smiled. He mellowed, instantly a man at peace with the world. Why, she was only a wisp of a thing! Her appearance belied her essence. Dreading the thought of someone picking on her, he wished she looked as tough as she really was and wondered what she would be without her tenacity. But a Katherine without that spirit of hers, that relentless drive and capability, was not something he could fathom.

"And there it is," he thought with a certain sadness. Shaking his head, he was persuaded that being sad on such a beautiful day would be the height of foolishness. Intent on raising his spirits, he said to Peter sitting beside Katherine, "join in and give your sister some support!"

Shaking his head, Peter replied: "If it's all the same to you Dad, I'd rather listen to James Taylor." And he gave his sister a look to say she was incorrigible, softened thereafter by an affectionate wink.

They drove east through North Carolina, through forests of green and blue trees, went past idyllic meadows and fields, and depending on fortune, horses too. What they saw was familiar; this was home after all. Yet, familiarity was not permitted to dull their senses.

On occasion they drove past roadside stalls selling fruit and vegetables. The stalls were pleasing to the eye. The harvest was plentiful. Testament to the fact, numerous baskets filled to the brim with produce, where the eye spied succulent peaches, melons, corn, tomatoes and all such. Though the stalls tempted, they did not stop. Their destination, by comparison, summoned them forcefully, much to the disappointment of those manning the stalls; the vendors to look up with expectation as their car drove by.

At the turn of the hour, a deep male voice interrupted the music to broadcast the latest news and the weather forecast. Confirmation of clear weather in the Outer Banks cheered them. Known for being fickle, one could hardly pin down the weather on the barrier islands – that it would be obliging made them very happy.

To prolong the good cheer of the announced fine weather, the disc jockey said: "For all you good folks out there, here's something from U2 ... Beautiful day." Peter grinned. Katherine stuck her tongue out at him and to his dismay began to sing along.

"Good day for a hunt!" Alexander erupted with a sparkle in his eyes, making Peter forget the jibe intended for his sister as he responded excitedly, "we are in for a real blast, man," sounding now every inch a man from the Carolinas as he beamed at his siblings.

Richard feigned enthusiasm. With the sea fast approaching, his stomach had developed painful knots sapping him of energy. And he felt his capacity for practical reasoning was in danger too. What else could explain why he believed it safe to let them go alone? When they doubtlessly depended on him. But soon after, he judged this reasoning rather lame. Unlike Jane who could stay at home, his only way really, was to be here with them.

Putting an end to his restraint, he pointed out the sea as it came into view, even though he knew everyone would have spotted it by now. His, happened to be a family of consummate observers – observers mind, with an educated eye. And if asked what they looked for, their answer would be: "Something out of the norm, something out of place." They kept their eyes peeled for any sign of a threat, bearing in mind that the brain was not fool proof. Sometimes it made mistakes. And there was too, the matter of the conscious and subconscious; they hoped that when the conscious wandered, which it was prone to do, and did not register stimuli as it ought, the subconscious would warn them to that effect. Aware that the subconscious was subtle, most of their training was tailored to strengthening their ability to wise up to this subtlety, to the schemes of the subliminal mind.

They crossed the bridge to East Lake and soon after another one over to Manteo. From Manteo it would be south now all the way to Hatteras Island. The thought of Moonbeam waiting for them at the marina sparked joy in Richard. A solid beauty, with every attention paid to her safety, she was a wonder to navigate. At first glance she was only a boat, a mere chattel, and he felt that his exhilaration went overboard. "I am compensating for something," he resolved sadly.

Arriving at the marina, Richard parked the car in front of the attendant's office. Determined to see them off without reservation, he stepped out with a flourish.

"Hello Trevor, how are you?" Richard greeted the man who walked out to him.

"Can't complain, not on day like this," he replied jovially, extending his hand. "I'm glad the very hot summer days are behind us. I prefer September, always have."

"No, that we can't," Richard said as he shook hands. "It's been a wonderful summer."

"You look well Richard."

Richard winked at him, saying, "and here's why," as his hand pointed to the children getting out of the car. "How is Chris?"

"He's doing fine. I'm going to be a grandfather in spring. Can you believe it?"

"Congratulations! That's wonderful news."

The children, now out of the car, greeted in unison, "hi, Trevor!"

Trevor opened his arms and embraced Katherine, then Peter, and finally Alexander. Releasing Alex, he looked him over and proclaimed: "You will never be too grown up to give some love to old Trevor, big little boy. Even when you become a father." And he laughed in the happy manner cherished by them all.

While he told them about their childhood friend Chris, Richard finished unloading the car, found the electric cord, plugged it in and handed the other end to Trevor: "I'm afraid I have to ask you once again – will you please charge the car for us, Trevor?"

"Of course, she'll be ready for you when you get back."

Bidding Trevor goodbye, the children picked up their luggage and marched the short distance to the berth occupied by Moonbeam. Named to pay homage to the moon for her influence on the oceans' tides, Moonbeam floated in her mooring with an air of confident charm and dignity, much the same as a swan, Richard thought. Her gleaming white hull contrasted strikingly with the dark blue sea.

And if she could speak, by way of welcoming them aboard Moonbeam would have said to Richard: "Enter ye who are wary, and I will give you rest." And to the others, "adventure awaits all those who enter in that spirit."

They stepped aboard, each with a spirit peculiar to them, with their own unique hopes and aspirations, yet bound to the family unit by a sense of belonging and by traits passed down through the generations to ensure humankind's tenacious hold on life.

On board, each one felt a weight on their shoulders, a responsibility to their forebears, to whom they would say, "I am in your debt." To those whose DNA they had inherited.

Richard immediately went into the cockpit, followed by Alexander, intent on making sure they had all the provisions for the trip. Peter took the cooler into the galley and set about putting food into the fridge while Katherine brought in the bag with the diving gear, opened it and hung their wetsuits on the hooks by the cabin door. Retrieving two thermos flasks, she placed them on the counter and, opening one, poured coffee into mugs. She called out to her brothers to fetch theirs and brought a cup to her father. "Here you are Dad."

Her father looked up and was smitten by his daughter's cheerful disposition. Taking the cup from her, "I need this, thanks darling," he said, as his demeanour suddenly became grave.

Seeing the change, Kat said, "tell me...please."

"I am counting on you to be the sensible one," Richard appealed to her.

Her response was solemn: "I always am." She reached her arm around his neck reassuringly.

Guiding Moonbeam out of the marina, Richard was happy to have her by his side. Known for her fascination with boats, Katherine avidly watched as they glided past the moored boats. When they came to the last one, Richard slowed down to a snail's pace and she smiled with delight as Spright finally came into view. Her eyes gleamed at what, in her opinion, was the most handsome yacht on the planet – the Nautor's Swan 95. The knowledge that this magnificent Finnish beauty belonged to her and her brothers made her smile grow even wider.

"She looks well," her father said.

Katherine only smiled. Richard was grateful she chose to hold her tongue. Though the children had designs on both sailing and diving, he could only stomach one activity and so it was diving they had picked. In which case, Richard had insisted they take Moonbeam.

On the threshold of the open sea, Alexander walked into the cockpit to help his father plot their course. Katherine left them and joined Peter on the deck. She helped him bring food out to the table and soon after the siblings sat down to eat.

Seeing that they still had ample time on the boat, they ate at leisure. When satisfied, Alexander went inside to keep his father company. Much later, with the boat anchored, father and son walked out onto the deck.

Katherine went inside to change. Richard sat at the table and watched his sons get ready.

Reaching for the other flask, he prepared hot toddies, stood up and handed glasses to the children who had now joined him. Raising his glass, he proposed a toast: "Here's to keeping warm and to the best of both worlds."

"To the best of both worlds," his children repeated.

Placing their empty glasses on the table a moment later, they edged themselves to the railing.

Saying, "see you soon, Dad," they tipped into the sea. Richard quickly went to see, but there was no trace of them left.

3.   *Richard with time on his hands*

Gentle waves rocked Moonbeam. A brisk breeze rushing past finally scattered the lingering mid-morning clouds. With this unveiling, Richard observed that his was the only boat at sea. "An old man and the sea," he murmured softly. Caught off guard by the remark, his desire to challenge it made him stand tall, check his posture and in alarm ask: "When did I begin to consider myself old?" But was he old? "Far from it!" he exclaimed, "I am only sixty-five." The seed sown, persuasion to the contrary fell on deaf ears, however. Feeling old and forlorn without his children, his thoughts turned to Jane at home, also alone.

"My children should be here … here, on the boat with me," he voiced his dislike for waiting for them. In this mood Richard could not help feeling resentment at the hand dealt him. It was a difficult hand, a hand hard to make heads or tails of. "If wishes were horses..." Brought up short, he recognised the thought for the illusion it was and quickly banished it. In the beginning, when the children were born, he had had this very thought and he knew then, as he did now, that one could not ride a phantom.

Though the years had come with much worry and anxiety, Richard felt he had a handle on things. The family's circumstance, hardly ordinary, took its toll, however, and fear was ever only an arm's length away. The decisions to be made seemed to him never-ending. Resolved to remain positive, he reminded himself that, so far at least, he had not failed them. That ought to count for something. He looked ahead to what lay in store for his children now that their lives were once again in flux. The future was unseen; the anxiety this brought and his constant preoccupation with their safety was at times unbearable.

"Their very nature!" he reflected, "will I ever get used to it?"

Spurred on by his impatience with waiting for them, something deep within Richard stirred and roused his tethered emotions. Ensuing thoughts caused him great anxiety, after which he was incapable of coherent thought. In an attempt to regain control, he shifted focus and peered into the water in search of his children. He crossed over to the other side and looked there too, but they were not to be found. Looming before his eyes were all the things that could go wrong. Incoherency persisting, he panicked. Determined to suppress his emotional outburst and his fear he searched for a way to calm down and quickly resorted to poetry. Inspired by the vast Atlantic waters in his vicinity, in a quavering voice he quoted Mr T.S. Elliot, belting out: "Water, water, water everywhere, what a waste of water. Not a drop to drink."

An air of despondency rendered him incapable of reciting more. Overwhelmed, he was compelled to pace the length of Moonbeam's deck. Back and forth he marched to the beat of his very own drum, a lone man adrift. The act did not provide him the catharsis he hoped for. With hindsight, he admitted to choosing the wrong verse altogether. Mr Elliot's words, did not calm him, they made matters worse. Gazing at the surrounding waters did little to soothe him, leading him to recall a time when the ocean had lulled and pacified; when the smell of the sea alone had made him happy before he even set eyes on it.

Now in the depths of despair, "where did the magic go?" he mulled, knowing full well the question was rhetorical. As his resolve gave way, feeling drained of energy, Richard stopped his pacing and mumbled, "on the other hand, I am not getting any younger." Suddenly ravenous, he went into the cabin in search of food.

He wished his children would come back early. Only once before, off the coast of Louisiana, was he thus surprised. He remembered the thrill of seeing them back so soon. When he looked closely at them, however, he had noticed how pale and frightfully haggard the boys were. Filled with dread, "what happened out there?" he had asked. Being their father's children, they were not forthcoming. Jane had stood by with a look of horror on her face. And that was the last time she accompanied them.

Out on the deck, Richard put his plate on the table, sat down and took small bites of food in a manner that would have pleased his mother when he was a boy. "Here I go again," thinking it odd that, when anxious, his thoughts turned to her. His eyes lit up as he recalled her very pleasant face, with a chin now part of her neck. For years his mother had openly expressed her displeasure. As always, the progression to these thoughts was regret because his method of coping had wasted a great deal of time. Having insight common to them both, he now understood what she had experienced. With scant appreciation of his affairs, she lived out her days in the very house he grew up, not far from Huddersfield, in Yorkshire. Afforded every conceivable comfort, his, was a secure upbringing – reminiscent of a 'Swallows and Amazons' sort of childhood – in a large house perched on a hill overlooking the mill by the stream.

Memories of spending countless summer hours following his mother around her wondrous garden, marvelling at the magic she left behind, came to him. At the height of summer an abundance of blossoms had played host to butterflies and insects. Though eager for most 'visitors', she had been squeamish about snails. Her screams to have them removed from the garden always tickled him.

His repeated plea, "look, they are harmless," was of no help.

The image of his mother in the garden was something he could conjure up in the blink of an eye. Though she had shared many of her trade secrets, he only remembered the one about the clematis. "To succeed with this beautiful plant, you must keep its base well shaded," she had instructed. The strange thing about it though, was how quickly the creeper shot up towards the sun, winding and wrapping itself onto anything and everything on the way up.

"Why is that the case?" he wondered then, finding it odd that he had not given the matter any thought before, not even when he had shared the knowledge with Jane.

Strange too, was the fact that, even if he tried, he could not imagine his mother in any other setting but at home. It went without saying that he was grateful for the stability in her life. This, he was aware, had not always been the case for his family. And he recalled his father's stories about the hardships his ancestors encountered when they built the mill house. Their efforts had paid off, however, as did the textile mill, the source of the Hartley fortune. While their affluence hailed from textiles, over the years their business interests had diversified but, despite this success, the original Victorian mill and the manor in the village of Leyton had remained their family home.

He thought, if only she had taken his word and he remembered her pleading, "Richard, please stop avoiding me."

"Don't be absurd, Mother. Why would I avoid you?"

"I was hoping you would tell me why," she had pointedly challenged him on the telephone, her voice sharp and unyielding.

Admitting it would have been hurtful to her. God knew how much he wished to be forthright, but, while the children were young, he had to avoid her.

Beyond any doubt, her sixth sense had cautioned her that something was amiss. "Not knowing is killing me. How can I help if you insist on keeping me in the dark?" Offering him money she had said: "Jane will need a nanny." Having turned down involvement in the family business, Richard was in her eyes a pauper and his refusal of assistance was to her mind absurd. A family with triplets needed all the reinforcements in the world. She did not know how much doctors in America earned, but supporting three babies in England would try his ability to stay in pocket, even on a doctor's pay.

Though her argument was most certainly sound, Richard had held firm. "Let her think as she pleases," he had thought, still smarting from her disapproving of his career choice. Yet he couldn't help wondering why she wished to assist Jane, whom she after all blamed for their moving to America, even though it had been equally his decision. Sometimes his mother made no sense at all. Two weeks after the children were born, a nanny sent by his mother drove up to their house in a taxi. Richard sent the nanny back the very next day.

The hurt in her voice when they next spoke tormented him for a long time. Richard being her best-behaved child, made this upset even more difficult for her to comprehend. But she apologised for meddling, explaining that she was aware every generation had their own ideas on how best to raise their offspring. "The pressures of fatherhood get to most new fathers." He was not the first, nor would he be the last, dared she say, to be affected in this way. Every time they had spoken since, she had found something to justify his behaviour. He was, after all, her eldest and her heir. Missing him dearly, at the end of their conversations she would mournfully say: "Only, do come for a visit Richard, it would be so good to see you." Despite their unsettled practicalities she longed to see him.

Feeling a bit cheeky now, Richard thought that second-guessing him was something his mother had put to quite good use over the years; an endless supply of mind games, the very thing recommended for people her age. And she had indeed benefited; despite being well into her eighties, her mind remained sharp.

His jesting was short-lived, for he missed her a great deal. He relived the many pleasant evenings they had spent together, just the two of them, his father working mostly in London and his much younger sister and brother put early to bed. In those hours, he had divulged details on every aspect of his life; he had kept nothing from her. She had proved herself a great confidante. At the time, he couldn't have foreseen the need to keep a secret from her. He wished he could come clean and spare her any ill feeling and he abhorred the distance his secret had created.

Even so, through the years, his instinct to keep her in the dark had prevailed. Strangely, the thousands of miles between them became a source of comfort. Her travel, with few exceptions, was mainly to London by train and

Richard knew she would stay on her side of the Atlantic. Aware of her limitation, before they left England, she had made Richard and Jane promise to visit every summer and Christmas. Without fail, on every visit before the children were born, she had begged them to come home. Arguing with her was exhausting and he envied Jane's patience – she never took offence.

"Calm down Richard," Jane would say, "she is after all your mother." With no family ties of her own, his wife's meaning could not be mistaken.

Aware he merely killed time Richard excessively chewed the small mouthfuls he took. "My stomach will thank me," he said flippantly to himself, no longer willing to contemplate difficult matters. He poured himself a cup of coffee, stood up and went into the cabin in search of the reading material he had brought, in the hope of catching up with the news. He realised that the last time he had read something was the day before the children's arrival. Even in the week they spent in New York, he had not read a single page. The excitement of having them back in a few days had been enough for him.

"And yet, not once did I miss it." He chose a newspaper and sat down to read. After an hour, he took a pause to use the bathroom.

Back on deck, he viewed a boat at a distance heading his way. He watched the boat get closer and closer and when he was sure he could be seen, he waved to the people on board. Since the boat was emblazoned with Deep Sea Fishing on the side, Richard gathered its occupants were fisherman. Those who said people on the water were at their most friendly were right. The fishermen waved enthusiastically, and some waved their hats at him too. The hat waving reminded him to find his own, but he was rooted to his spot. A long time ago, he himself, was an avid fisherman. His mind on fishing, he remembered what he had heard on the news when the disaster in Fukushima happened. It was reported that the fisherman there did not go out anymore. But neither had he, not for an age. He had imagined their boats on fallow in the harbour, waiting. But, for how long would they wait?

The fishermen must have been waiting too. Very likely, no pier or harbour survived. He imagined the people evacuated and the boats reduced to wreckage. He had wondered too about the currents that licked the Fukushima coastline. How far out to sea did they go? "And that is the elephant in the room," something no one wanted to talk about and which, to him, was a bright red flag.

He imagined that the seas were wastelands and, in them, nothing to recommend, where jetsam and flotsam contaminated and choked the very life out of the waters. He shook his head, "what a tragedy." Recently, he had heard that the city was open once again to its residents. He felt sad for the people whose lives had been devastated. For years the scientists had insisted that nuclear energy was 'safe and clean', but how could one even begin to relate those words to what had happened there?

Around that time, two very large fish were found dead on the beach in San Francisco. Two very unusual specimens, that normally lived at a thousand meters deep. The incident had captured his attention and imagination. How many more were floating about in the sea? What lay between Japan and America except the sea?

He was emphatic: "Humankind is systematically poisoning the Earth. Her oceans, rivers, fields and atmosphere are chock-full of toxins. She is suffering from a chronic fever induced by the toxins and in order to cool down she perspires greatly and becomes dehydrated." Diagnosing her symptoms as her ailment was farcical. Identifying what plagued our planet as merely climate "change" was downright disingenuous. Besides, presenting the problem in such a vague and insurmountable term was only intended to bamboozle and incapacitate people. And the term "climate change" now sounded to his ear like a fairy tale.

Beyond any doubt, the wrong diagnosis prevailed because it suited the masters of humankind whose industries perpetrate the poisoning daily. These masters have hijacked governments so that, instead of serving the people, governments sided with industry at the *expense* of the people and, ultimately, our planet. When challenged, the reason most governments gave for supporting these industries was that they were "too big to fail." Earth was too big to fail!

He faulted his fellow world citizens for their naivety, for believing they were in control. Systems of government as they stood were not of the people; nor were they by or for the people. Considering diesel generators to be a viable backup for nuclear plants during a storm or disaster was the height of folly.

As custodians, human beings have failed Earth miserably and Richard charged them all with the greatest crime of negligence ever committed. They should have kept a closer watch! His thoughts were now imbued with a sense of urgency and, if privy to them, one might have sensed desperation too. Contemplating all these matters filled him with trepidation. "What a mess. And soon, unless we change, the oceans – our foremost source of oxygen – will cease to sustain life. They are fast becoming wastelands."

He imagined people saying to him: "Who are you to talk?" Yes, it was only human to challenge and question. For Richard, discourse on the seminal issues of the day was always a noble undertaking; if not a duty, one to be encouraged. As far as he was concerned, every living soul ought to be chilled to the marrow by what was happening to the planet and agitating tirelessly to save it. Consider those who drank contaminated water every day and breathed toxic air and the fact that virtually all processed food on grocery shelves these days is laced with high fructose syrup. If workers on banana plantations were bearing children without reproductive organs or were themselves becoming sterile after years of chemical spraying, should bananas grown on those plantations make their way to our children? Children who reached for a banana on the way home from school and peeled it with their teeth? Children who arrived at home only to be faced with food that spent life in confinement, was force-fed to mature early and given antibiotics to keep it alive in hostile conditions.

Can the human body cope with modern day living? When we are transported while seated, feasting, as we do, on food grown in fields leached of nutrients? With the demands people placed on their internal organs by the constant nibbling and the sipping of something sugary all day long? Have our organs evolved to cope with this pattern of consumption? Was the pseudo food served nowadays fit for human consumption and good health? At this level of domestication, what were our chances? "And more to the point, as a race, are we to survive these changes?" Richard questioned.

Sadly, the answer for Richard was that the human body was heavily taxed and good health was becoming a rarity. With poor health, people's senses were dulled and their instinct for survival greatly diminished. This explained their passivity in the face of such grave danger. And if there was anyone out there who thought that they were sitting pretty, then he was afraid he would have to tell them to think again.

"If only the sea did not have such a hold on them," he lamented. The fishing boat having fallen out of sight now, he sat down to read the paper, which, shortly thereafter fell on his face.

When his children returned there were bits of newspaper strewn all over the boat and their father's face and arms were as red as a lobster's, there, where he slept.

Roused from his slumber by Peter's voiced disapproval of his attempt to roast himself in the sun, Richard drowsily stood up. "This is going to hurt Dad," his concerned son said, as he led him into Moonbeam's cabin.

Katherine tut-tutted at him while generously rubbing aloe gel into the affected areas.

"Mum won't like this," she said with much conviction.

"You are right, of course," Richard answered, smiling happily as if he had been paid a compliment. Inside he was flying high, as high as a kite would out here in the constant breeze. "They are back, my brood is back," he repeatedly said to himself as relief and joy flowed through him, right into his very scorched arms and cheeks.

The gel application completed, Richard stood up, looked out to the deck and observed, "I see you've had no luck today?"

"Nope, not today," Peter answered.

Laughing heartily, "nobody in their right mind would say you were in need of more treasure."

Peter and Katherine chuckled at their father's response, while Alexander looked on with a smirk.

"All right children, go and rinse the sea off." Richard reached for the ignition and started the boat.

4.   The sermon

Timing their arrival with precision, the Hartley car pulled into St Mark's parking lot as the church bell intruded on the serenity of a Sunday morning. Bathed all night by rain, the day awoke bright and crisp with a bite in the air. Richard led them from the main entrance up the nave and along the way they smiled at people who caught their eye. The smiles to greet them were today even wider, it being the day of the harvest lunch.

When seated, out of force of habit, Jane sent the children an enquiring glance. No longer needed she worry about her children crawling under the pew to play hide and seek; nor was there need for her to anxiously count the minutes before Miss Helen, the Sunday school teacher, fetched them. Shaking her head in a manner suggesting she had forgotten herself, Jane turned to her husband and lightly nudged him with her elbow. His response was the knowing smile reserved for occasions when he could read her like a book: "This is how it ought to be; family should be together."

They were barely seated when the organist commenced playing, prompting the congregation to stand up in song and welcome their minister. Peter looked at Katherine, but today she did not sing. He smiled at her approvingly. Alexander saw him smile and he too smiled at his siblings. And when they looked up, their lively minister beamed from the pulpit.

All those who attended St Mark's agreed they left the Sunday service feeling the love of an inspired fellowship. Theirs was a congregation with a confidence and warmth to move everyone and anyone. To this end members eagerly tasked themselves with arranging social events for their fellowship. And their minister was happy to leave them to it. Perhaps this was the reason most congregants offered their service and attended worship regularly. There was nothing to shy away from at St Mark's. In God's own good time they cared in equal measure for each other and the community outside their fellowship.

The reverend's methods they all agreed worked well, but none quite as well as his sermons, the singular purpose of which was to fortify faith. "Is He not, after all, the Creator of everything that was ever made?" he would solemnly ask. Reverend Brent recited the third verse from the first chapter of John frequently to his flock to emphasise this belief: "All things were made through Him, and without Him nothing was made, that was made." For this reason, more than any other, Jane had great respect for the man. The verse moved her very essence and, had the reverend been privy, he would have given himself a pat on the shoulder.

"Everything that was made," Jane reflected, and her thoughts on the matter, like charity, began at home. Yes, that would include her children, her wonderful boys and girl. And there was her husband of many years, Richard. And, as if that were not enough, she had also been blessed with her home, her hens and her garden. The garden delighted and calmed her even as it demanded her care. Care in her opinion, amounting to far less in terms of labour and effort than the many benefits she received in return. God wished His children to live in the peace and calm of a garden. Removed from the garden, they were restless and out of touch with their Creator. They would have no peace out there, in the wilderness. No one, least of all Jane, should have any doubt on this matter.

Jane's attention, through no fault of her own, drifted from the reading of the gospel. The reader's voice was much too soothing to captivate her on a day when she was anxious about her luncheon. Her spirit flitted away and found its way home. In the house, it wandered here and there, skimming through the rooms and finally moved to the kitchen where her caterer, Jackson, and his crew were preparing lunch for her friends. It checked on the progress there and was quietly pleased.

Presently, the minister walked to the pulpit to begin the sermon. Jane's spirit returned and, in anticipation, she and her fellow believers sat taller in their seats. This was the reason they had come: to have their cups filled.

Holding forth on his sacred duty, the reverend commenced, "though unseen, God is real. We have faith and, therefore, have no need to lay eyes on Him. But here's the clincher: our forefathers witnessed Him in the flesh and have passed on that legacy to us. Therefore, I can stand here with confidence and proclaim that every day God is at work around us. Did our Lord Jesus Christ not say to Thomas: 'Blessed are those who did not see me and yet have believed'?"

On matters spiritual, Reverend Brent's demands on his congregation were exacting. He perceived his teaching vital to their spiritual well - being and to their salvation. Losing any of them was something he couldn't afford. Imploring them to pay attention to God's work happening daily all around them he reassured, "every day the sun rises in the east and sets in the west. The seasons come and go with regularity. Even when you sleep at night, your own breath is regular. God holds you in the palms of His hands."

He reminded them that God was merciful, that He was a God of second chances. Reverend Brent did not like it when Christians beat up on themselves. "Don't doubt Him," he pleaded. "Doubt is the ploy of the enemy. If you ask for forgiveness, God will not deny you. Be grateful you have Him on your side. Gratitude," he added, "is a sure sign of faith. We all know that all good things come from God. When we place our faith and trust in Him, we have nothing to fear. Our hearts will be at peace. And when we are at peace, brothers and sisters, we are with God. God knows what you need."

Slowly moving from the pulpit, he walked to the edge of the altar to get closer to his flock and stood in front of them silently, willing all eyes in the church to meet his. The air was filled with a certain tension, a palpable strain that Reverend Brent tugged at purposefully. An experienced hand, he only loosened the tension just before they snapped. It was important that they remember this.

"Will God give you a snake when you ask Him for a fish?"

"No! God will give us a fish," the congregation replied, following their response with a short outburst of laughter, undoubtedly brought on by their need to let off steam.

"That's right! He'll give you a fish to sustain you."

For fear of revealing the emotion etched on their faces, when the family stood up to sing, they looked not at each other, but at the altar. The sermon had touched a raw nerve and had left them with mixed feelings, much like the field in the parable everyone knew so well, where the weeds grew side-by-side with the crop of wheat. Though they had much to be thankful for, sometimes they found it hard to be grateful.

"It was grace that taught my heart to fear and grace my fear relieved," the congregation now sang as one. Suddenly, the line leapt out and came to life for Alexander. His spirit sensed the revelation to come. If only it could be revealed to his feeble mind. Grace, they sang, both taught fear and relieved it, too. Of the siblings, he was the one to have seen real fear and he knew fear to be a double-edged sword. In situations of grave danger, he had seen frightened men accomplish unimaginable feats. It struck him hard then, perhaps harder than ever before, that fear was ever-present; always some sort of fear one had to contend with. Remembering then that the man who wrote the song was going blind when he wrote it, his heart quivered.

"Such faith," he thought, "sufficient to make a blind man see; enough to bring a man to balance." Then he himself saw it, a credit and a debit entry as if on a balance sheet. And he understood, "in life, one must avail themselves of both kinds of grace: the kind that inspires fear and the kind that relieves it."

"Isn't that wonderful?" he reflected, remembering a favoured Bible verse: "the fear of the Lord is the beginning of all wisdom."

5.   An open book

Midway into the hallway, Jane raised a hand to stop those behind her, breathed in deeply, then turned, and with delight smiled at her family. The scent of flowers gently clung to the air.

"Can you smell that?" she asked, as she let them pass.

"What a lovely scent, Mother," Peter said, kissing her cheek, convinced she would not tire of asking them this question. Alex and Katherine smiled indulgently.

"My dear, you have outdone yourself once again," Richard agreed as he repeated her motto: "To entertain well, indulge all senses." And they all giggled.

Jane put away her Sunday shoes, stepped into her slippers and went into the dining room. Situated on the west end of the ground floor, the room took up the whole width of the house. Since access to the garden was all-important to Jane, French windows covered the length of the three outer walls. The six round tables set for the occasion were elegant. After picking up a few straying petals from the tables, she declared the room in a fit state to receive guests and in admiration, stood back to take in the scene.

"It's really quite charming in here," she happily thought.

Observing her guests having a wonderful time due to her honest effort was immensely gratifying for Jane. After the family was settled, her decision had been as good as made; she would host a harvest luncheon for the entire congregation. And since that event had been such a success Jane's addition of an Easter luncheon to St Mark's calendar, was welcomed by all. And in between the two big occasions, she entertained smaller groups for lunch, tea or dinner when it suited.

In recent years, however, attendance at her luncheons had dwindled. In the beginning, even with a miracle, she could not fit all her guests into the dining room, and she had had to hire a marquee to ensure adequate space for all those who came to the 'Hartley Inn'. Nowadays, the only people to regularly attend church were the elderly, and lately, hardly any new faces could be discerned. Sadly, the ranks of the venerable members had shrunk. Their loss was heartbreaking. St Mark's was no longer a large, vibrant fellowship.

Though she only admitted to it grudgingly, there was an ulterior motive behind her decision to entertain. Jane wished that her family would be perceived as an open book. Intent on living the rest of her life in Pinewood, it was imperative that they assimilated into the local community. In her heart of hearts, however, she knew they would not fit in, not as such. But in their circumstances, being seen as just another family would be an honest-to-goodness boon.

Keenly aware that moving to a small town was a delicate endeavour, Jane understood the importance of putting her best foot forward. Long before her family moved into their house, she had carefully cultivated relationships with her new neighbours. When she oversaw the renovation of the house, every business in town that could be of service was involved in some way. Placing great value on local knowledge and skills, she chose builders from Pinewood.

Rich in the furniture-making traditions of North Carolina, handed down to him by his ancestors, she commissioned the local carpenter, Joshua, to fit out the house with bespoke furnishings. His craftsmanship was impressive; the man was truly a master. She was especially pleased with his fitted closets and bookcases. Without question, however, his masterpiece was the winding oak staircase he fashioned to replace the rotted, unsafe spectacle they had inherited.

The seamstress in the main street made her curtains. Pinewood Pools extended and turned their pool into an indoor one. Later, when the know-how was available, with Peter's assistance, they replaced the water filter with a reed grass-cleansing system. The local nursery sourced the largest dogwood trees obtainable and transplanted a multitude along their lengthy, narrow driveway.

"They are thoroughly decent," she had thought of "her people" then, while craving familiarity.

Her family was well liked but, as was the case with matters of affection, not everyone found them agreeable. And, so it was that certain Pinewood inhabitants had yet to make up their minds about this new family. Even after so many years they considered them strangers still.

"What do we actually know about them? I mean, they're not from around here, or anywhere near here for that matter. Besides, they are English," some were heard to say.

Though quite aware of these sentiments, the family felt safe and assured in this community. Pinewood really was the sort of town one dreamed of when one thought of moving to the country. Its sleepy charm was infectious.

Remembering herself, Jane forsook her introspection, made her way to the utility room and vigorously washed her hands. Donning an apron on her way into the kitchen, once there, she demanded, "tell me what to do Jackson."

"I'm afraid you are late," Jackson grinned cheerfully.

Katherine, in the hallway, overheard and counselled, "Mum, chef does not want you in his kitchen. Take the hint while he is being nice."

Jane laughed heartily and mused to herself, "quite right. But to think that when she had started out so long ago, she had done all the cooking herself!"

"Perhaps that's not quite correct," she remembered stifling a laugh. Her dear friend Monique, for one, would not take kindly to the notion. She had had her help plus her clear recommendation to move to Pinewood.

6.   The luncheon

Driving east on Madison Road, the main street in town, where they lived next to Benton's Food Store, Duane and Hannah Benton made their way to Oak Leaf Farm. Benton's, the most reputable store in Pinewood, had been in Duane's family for three generations and to Duane's delight the big supermarkets found Pinewood's population too small to be worth their while. The pickings, they had determined, would never be more than lean there. Duane was still fearful of the future and, to survive the competition if ever it came, he had shifted his focus to foods sourced locally and grown organically.

At the same time, his brother, Alan, had converted his farm into a pesticide-free vegetable and fruit farm to supply Benton's, amongst others. Alan now subscribed to the ancient, biblical practice of fallowing farmland for seven years, believing it the only way to sustainably replenish his farmland's soil. In his mind, no chemical fertiliser in existence could possibly contain all the God-given minerals and nutrients required for healthy soil and, in turn, healthy people.

Hannah managed the section of Benton's that made preserves and relishes from the excess fruit and vegetables. Nothing ever went to waste at Benton's.

Fearful of stagnating, Duane was constantly in search of unique stock. Striving to maintain a sense of novelty as a service to his customers, he often tempted them into trying new foods, encouraging them to explore and challenge their palates: "And why not," he would reply. "Isn't variety the spice of life?" Fancying himself an educator, when pitching his wares, he'd delicately pose the question, "can we really talk about the quality of life and neglect to mention healthy food?" His efforts were paying off. The store's reputation was growing, as was, the demand for its ever-widening assortment of goods. Now, patrons from as far away as Chapel Ridge frequented Benton's. He hoped and trusted they would remain loyal.

The pair travelled in silence. Preoccupied with thoughts of the Hartley house, though gazing out the window towards the idyllic town beyond, Hannah saw none of it. She puzzled over the lovely scent in the house, every time she had visited. Though convinced the source were the flowers, she could not shake the notion that there was something else besides. Simply asking Jane would have solved the riddle for her but, for some inane reason, she couldn't bring herself to.

"How does Jane manage it all?" Hannah wondered with admiration. The table usually set simply, but just so, eloquently foretold of the pleasures to come. The music played was chosen to permit the guests to sit back, lower their shoulders and relax. Their hosts were beyond reproach; every guest was made to feel very important but, with no fuss to speak of. "If only I could throw a Thanksgiving dinner party to her standard," she thought as a moan slipped out.

"What was that honey?" Duane asked.

"Never mind."

The couple drove past St Marks, one of the three churches in the small town assembled neatly in the centre. The Catholics and the Baptists were also represented. All three places of worship had white steeples reaching high into the sky, giving the town a picturesque prospect. Further down, towards the end of Madison Road, they passed kempt, white picket fence homes with charming gardens. The pride people took in their town was obvious wherever the eye roamed.

Soon after they found themselves on the outskirts of Pinewood and, at a distance, sheltered by a mature red oak forest stood Oak Leaf Farmhouse. Parking in front of the house, the Benton's stopped to admire Jane's garden before strolling to the door.

Richard ushered them into the expansive hallway where Alex waited to serve arriving guests delectable drinks and his mother guided them breezily through the dining room and onto the porch where the other guests had casually convened.

As she walked through, Hannah noted the dining room was transformed. On this occasion the room had six round tables to accommodate thirty guests. "And today we are to have our very own private restaurant," she thought smiling.

On the porch, the guests chatted animatedly. Around them, the results of Jane's green fingers, evident in the pots and tubs and the fetching autumn garden, provided the perfect backdrop. In this delightful setting, the courtesy they paid each other was heightened.

Hannah cheerfully greeted the reverend and his wife, Joyce, then left the talking to her husband in order to look around. In all the years her hosts had lived here, her curiosity about them had not waned. In the beginning, she had only come to get a glimpse of the house. Picturing the family seated on the linen sofas with three small children, she couldn't imagine them relaxed. She had given the sofas a six-month lease on life.

When Sarah and Frank Clark approached her, Hannah stilled her roving eye to talk to Sarah who shared her curiosity about their hosts. But because the Clark twins, Melinda and Brenda, had left for the University of Virginia earlier in the month, propriety demanded that she enquire after their well-being instead ... at least for now.

Sarah looked distraught at their mention, "I miss them terribly and I worry far too much," she confided, her eyes tearing just a tad.

Frank assured her, "we'll visit them next weekend," and drew her close to him. "That will be a lot of fun. I'm sure everything is fine." For his wife's benefit, he quickly changed the subject to Hannah's son, Duane Junior, who lived in New York. "How's Duane doing?" he asked, knowing full well the mention of her only child would set Hannah off. Talking about Duane assuaged her longing for him.

While sharing titbits about her son, Hannah's latent curiosity suddenly arose and attracting Sarah's attention, urgently asked if the de Paris had arrived.

The French couple were Catholics, who nonetheless, were invited to the luncheons. Befuddled by the close friendship between their hosts and the Catholic pair, both women were hard pressed to avoid passing judgement. They blamed this friendship for their failed attempts to get closer to Jane and Richard and could not fathom their hosts' desire to befriend Catholics.

Had they taken the time to get to the root of their preconceived notions, they might have arrived at a different conclusion, one without unashamed bias. For who could tell what an unencumbered mind might devise? There were those who would associate genius with such a mind. But so far, no circumstance had yet persuaded the two good ladies to part with their bias.

Presently, Hannah whispered to Sarah, "here she comes," as their gazes found Monique walking beside Jane, in impeccable clothes, hinting at her desirability, in a manner they envied, but would be loath to admit. Monique, the women had noticed, made their husbands stand tall when she approached. It was said that this awareness didn't endear her to them. As for the reverend's earnest teaching on the value of loving one's neighbour, well, she was not their neighbour, not really.

Hannah had observed that her husband used a special voice for 'Madame de Paris' whenever they spoke. This irritated her terribly. As usual, her head to toe inspection of Monique left her peeved. A quick glance at Duane revealed that he wasn't yet aware of the new addition to their party. Returning her attention to Monique, she saw Katherine embrace her godmother.

Holding her at arm's length for a better look, Monique exclaimed, "très, très jolie!" and hugged her once more. Peter joined them and Hannah, still listening in, was reminded that the Hartley children were fluent in French.

In the meantime, Richard invited the guests to be seated. When they were comfortably settled, Reverend Brent, standing, said grace. "Bless these gifts, Lord, and those who partake in them. We thank You for the nourishment we are about to receive. We pray for the will to resist temptation and ask Your guidance in all matters. It is in the name of your son, Jesus Christ, that we pray."

And those seated responded: "Amen."

When seated, with a nod and a smile, the minister acknowledged Monique on his right and then Hannah on his left.

Monique smiled at him when he again looked her way, and teasingly said: "Thank you for saying grace. It was comforting and, happily, not too long." The minister laughed with delight. It was not every day that people spoke freely to him. He felt sure she would treat him like any other; with her there was to be none of that reverent nonsense people hid behind when they spoke to him.

"The food can't wait, and neither can I," he replied still laughing while thinking, "well, better this, than what I am used to." He remembered being seated next to her on another occasion, but it was a while ago and long enough for him to forget how refreshing her candour was. Jane was meticulous about moving her guests around. His eyes met Pierre's seated across and he gave him a nod too. He would have welcomed being seated beside him. Pierre was a lot of fun and the wine he brought from his vineyard for these occasions, was out of this world. A good wine enhanced every meal. Even the good Lord Himself recognised the importance of wine at a party. It was significant enough after all to be the subject of his very first miracle; the miracle requested by his mother at the wedding in Cana.

He thanked God for the French couple. God forbade he should take anyone or anything for granted. A plate was placed before him and beholding the meal, he thanked God for it once more as well as the hands that had prepared it. He counted it a blessing to call Jane and Richard friends. They were such wonderful people.

Looking around the table, he saw that not everyone had been served. He would wait. Seeking diversion to make the waiting easier, he had the thought: "My flock is oblivious to the rigours of delivering a good sermon. Not only is it trying, it's also exhausting."

Afterwards, he felt drained and was famished. It seemed to him strange that talking should make one so hungry. Sunday lunch was, therefore, an essential meal for him. Feeling his hunger pangs more strongly than ever, he registered how easily the body overpowered the mind, as Jesus' warning to the disciples came clearly to him: "The mind is willing, but the body is weak." His eyes, one of the many parts of his body darted at his plate once more, as his empty stomach rumbled. Lifting them away quickly, he saw Hannah pick up her cutlery, "here we go," he whispered to himself as he dug in.

"Bon appétit," Monique said.

With his mouth full, a nod was all he could manage. But after he swallowed, he turned to Hannah and wished her the same. Pierre's wine was poured into his glass. He gave it a gentle swirl by the stem, lifted the bowl to his nose and then placed his lips to the glass's edge. A smile crossed his face.

"Now this is superb," he remarked with reverence after his first sip.

"You like it?" Pierre asked.

"Very much."

Pierre told him about the grape, about its German origins and how he had obtained it from Missouri. "Missouri," he informed the reverend with mischief, "believe it or not was once the wine capital of America."

Seeing his surprise, he nodded with vigour, uttering, "I am happy it's thriving in my vineyard." And he laughed passionately as the emotion in his eyes swung like a pendulum from passion to mischief, in a dizzying back and forth.

The minister wondered at his enthusiasm and was amazed at how he kept it up. "I can learn something from Pierre," he thought with humility. Often now, his enthusiasm failed him.

Remarking on the food, Monique said: "This starter is simply delicious!"

Pierre smiled at her with mischief and something else besides; something rather private that made the minister face's colour as he averted his glance, thinking it wise to focus his attention on his plate. Perhaps, he had said enough for today.

Duane proudly informed everyone at the table that the artichokes and fennel for the starter came from Benton's.

With the starter cleared away, pasta with the freshest tomato and basil sauce ever made, in Duane's opinion, was served. It too, was delicious. Fittingly, conversation ebbed as the guests' attention turned to the food. But for the mild clicking of utensils into a persistent background symphony, a silence had descended on the room. The plates were cleared. As desert was served, conversation picked up. Fig tart was consumed with relish, accompanied by a light and sweet dessert wine, another offering from Pierre's vineyard. The conversation was now on a marked upswing.

Mellowed by good food and wine, the guests endeavoured to further enjoy themselves. Pushing their chairs back for better legroom, they lifted their glasses to be refilled.

And, as was their wont, their stomachs immediately set to work extracting energy from their contents and in the process ignited a glow there. When the glow caught, the warmth slowly spread to their limbs and loosened them up, as well as their tongues, permitting them to converse freely with each other. Abuzz with talk and laughter, the room hummed. It was suddenly a must that they all get a word in. And they talked about themselves and all those things they held dear.

Duane talked about Benton's. "Think about it, Pierre. Wouldn't it be nice if I sold your outstanding wine?"

Pierre laughed, "Duane, you know the winery is just a hobby for me. I'm a tailor. I want every man to have a suit tailored to his exact dimensions, preferably fashioned out of cashmere. A suit cut to bring out the best in him."

Duane countered with excitement, "imagine," he said, "that man in your suit, feeling at his very best and drinking your excellent wine. Picture it please, Pierre."

"Speaking of which, did you bring the suits for Alex and Peter?" Monique cut in. Then, apologetically, "sorry for interrupting, Duane. I was supposed to remind him before we left home, but I forgot."

Duane responded in the voice he used only for Monique, "I understand, no worries."

On hearing her husband talk this way, Hannah grimaced. "Men...it's hard to know what to do with them," she expressed in her mind as she watched Monique. But, how could she fault her? The woman only had eyes for her husband. Had she not a moment ago witnessed the bond between them?

"Yes, ma chérie, I have the suits," Pierre said.

"Good, then my time at the party won't be interrupted," Monique said laughing. Doted on by her husband, she knew full well he would have been the one to fetch the suits. A midwife, with her own practice, she joked then about her fear of being called away if someone went into labour. "Sometimes they go into labour at the most inconvenient times, I must say." She laughed heartily, not in the least sounding as though she would mind the interruption.

"Perhaps you should retire," Pierre said with mischief.

Looking at her husband in mock horror, she admonishingly shook a finger at him saying, "what will I do while you tailor suits and tend your vineyard?"

Duane shook his head in disbelief. The Europeans in Pinewood were such a taxing lot. Why could they not recognise opportunity when it presented itself? Jane was the same; she would not sell him any of her hens.

"At least think about it, Pierre," he implored.

Pierre laughed, "dear Duane, you are asking too much of an old man. You make me wish I were younger."

"You old? Nonsense!" Duane impulsively blurted out. But when he recalled how old Pierre was, he chastised himself. Being such a vibrant man, one easily overlooked his age; he was seventy-five and not a day younger. His wife's youth certainly rubbed off on him.

Hannah cut in to speak about her son. "Duane is coming home for Thanksgiving and guess what? He's bringing a friend, a girl."

"What? Why didn't you tell me?" Duane exclaimed.

Among friends they had found empathy and a kinship. A sensation hard to describe gripped them all and their minds, momentarily relieved of the burden of stress, ceased to judge. They cast their frailties and prejudices to the side; there was nothing to fear, really. In touch with their humanity, the de Paris ceased to be Catholics and became firm friends. As for the Hartley family, they might as well have all been born in Pinewood; they considered them family. In this liberated mind-set, their promise seemed to them well within reach and the feeling went to their heads. It was euphoric.

"What an excellent party!" they exclaimed, as the conversation rose to a crescendo and for a while admirably held its own, rendering time insignificant. How could time – or any earthly care – possibly matter now?

At the sight of his wife, children and friends enjoying themselves, "what a thing it is to live in the moment," Richard surmised with glee.

Ever mindful of her guests, Jane looked for the tell - tale signs she had come to know so well, the moment when her guests sought more comfort and she suggested leaving the dining table.

As soon as she had suggested it, Hannah quickly rose from her chair, made a beeline for the living room, found a sofa beside a French window and sank into it slowly, while heaving a sigh of contentment. Other women followed suit, but not the men. Wishing to be left to their own devices, they edged themselves towards the spacious porch and once there adopted attitudes of comfort and relaxation.

Commanded by Jane to go outside, when Jackson joined the men they clapped and gathered to congratulate the chef. Jane and Peter went out to them with a tray of coffee, more wine and glasses. Richard and Pierre served their friends; the first glass of wine now went to the man whose cooking had delighted them all.

As Pierre sipped his wine, he remembered that the suits for Alexander and Peter were still in the car. Beckoning Peter, he asked him to fetch them. Peter obliged and returned momentarily with the garments. The men asked to see them and then demanded that the boys show them off. Alex and Peter left, to shortly return suited looking very dapper, winning everyone's admiration.

Duane whistled as his left hand unconsciously went up to his waist. Lately, his expanding girth had prevented him from wearing his own custom-made suit, a gift from Pierre to mark his twentieth wedding anniversary. The man was afflicted with a flamboyant generosity. All the men in the room had been presented with a suit to mark a special milestone. A year after he received his own, when he found out from Duane junior how much people paid for Pierre's suits, he had nearly fainted. It was easy to appreciate the expense; in his suit he felt like any man's equal. He could walk into a room anywhere, head held high. Yearning now with some frustration to lose weight, he said: "I wish I fit into my suit."

Reverend Brent said, "mine is tight, too. Why don't we do something about it, Duane?"

"Yes, let's. Shall we walk or run?"

"Let's start by walking. Small steps."

"On which days?"

"Mondays and Wednesdays work for me."

Shortly thereafter the men, who could not resist Pierre's fantabulous stories, demanded his attention.

Clearing his throat: "What is the most important question a tailor asks his customer when taking their trouser measurements?" he asked.

The men looked blankly at each other and Pierre feigned great disappointment. The men, of course, knew the answer but preferred the way he told it.

With comical politeness, "does Monsieur dress to the right or to the left?" he asked. "Do you know what one of them said to me?"

"It depends on who is asking!" the men answered, erupting into howling laughter.

"For the sake of your comfort sir, it is your tailor asking," he recounted.

"In that case, it's to the right," Pierre mimicked the customer and joined in the laughter. He had no understanding for people who wished to complicate matters. This was not a trick question and being evasive about such a practical and uncomplicated matter was incomprehensible to him. Was life not demanding enough as it was?

Pierre knew there were all kinds of men out there. Like the suits he tailored, they too came in all shapes and sizes. He had met men of good character, in possession of a conscience, as well as those without. He was acquainted with rich men who swooped in with helicopters and jets to acquire his suits. Among them were men addicted to the limelight, but also those who prized their privacy. Some came for the sole purpose of being able to say de Paris himself had tailored their suit. Yet they lacked true appreciation for his craft. Nor did they recognise that a bit of his very soul was invested in each garment he made. These were not the kind of men able to see either within themselves or beyond themselves. In such case, being one at liberty, he would decide that none of his time would be available.

Sometimes his suit bestowed on a fellow the desire to carry themselves, well, reminded them to stand up tall, check their posture and recognise that they were men of equal worth. This was for Pierre the very best of outcomes. Yes, a suit indeed had the power to restore a man's dignity. And yet a man dressed in only one of two ways, either to the left or to the right. What it really came down to was that all men were the same species.

These thoughts moved Pierre, leading him to propose the following toast: "To the truth and the salvation it brings."

"To salvation," the men replied.

In time, the guests spread out to different parts of the house and the garden, finding company where they pleased. Though scattered, considerate attention was not far away. Their hosts and Jackson's staff made sure of it.

Taking their leave, the guests admitted it to themselves once again that the Hartley family were indeed good people. Every aspect of the luncheon had been enjoyable, and they felt that the next time would not come soon enough.

7. Departure

Jane, Richard and their son Alexander were gathered in the kitchen. Rid of all trace of function, a sense of relaxation now prevailed there. Before they went upstairs to finish packing, Peter and Katherine had washed the dishes from their light supper at eight o'clock. The kitchen counters gleamed.

Now at hand, the time of day when there was but one thing left to be done, and that was to retire for the night. Yet none of them were eager to end the day. On the side table beside Jane's armchair, the coffee, well past that perky aromatic state when everyone must have a cup, was ignored. In silence they basked in the warmth of the crackling fire in the hearth, as the leaping flames enticed and subdued the eye, rendering the mind tranquil. In time, the flames tapered and licked and soon after began to flicker, reminding them that the fire needed tending. With that, the spell was broken, and their faculties reinstated.

"This is how it will be," Jane thought, "once again as before, Richard and I will be sitting here contemplating our children, wondering how they're getting on."

Looking at Alexander, seated across from her, her mouth curved into a tiny smile. He was a sight for sore eyes. "Look at him," she thought with swelling pride beholding her eldest son sitting tall beside his father. She thought of asking him to throw a log on the fire but decided against it.

Then her mind turned to Peter and to the lorry arriving the week before to collect his belongings for shipment. Witnessing the excitement on his face she had just for a moment acquiesced: "Richard is right, if not in pursuit of their dreams, how else should a young person spend their youth?" With all her might, she tried to understand him. And there had been moments when she thought she had figured it out, but, when she fathomed the great distance his move entailed, she balked at his choice. Why go so far away when she was sure a marine biologist could be put to perfectly good use right here in North Carolina? He could have looked for work at the universities at Chapel Ridge and Durham, and even at one of the many firms in the Research Triangle. Keeping herself from stressing over how he was getting on would be difficult, to say the least, as she had never been to Norway.

Alex then asked if she would wake up to say goodbye.

"Of course, I'll wake up," she responded sharply. What an affront! Did he actually think she would get a wink of sleep tonight?

Alexander's eyes softened.

"Poor boy, I am being hard on him," she thought with regret, her face apologetic.

"It's just that, I will hear you when you wake up, so I might as well. Shall I make coffee?" she asked as her nurturing side took over just then.

"That will be lovely, Mum," Alex said smiling, knowing she would make the coffee just right. It would be the kind she made for traveling, robust, calculated to perk them right up and keep them alert when they left the house in the early hours.

"She is so predictable," he thought, finding this trait much to his liking. Leaving home without waving goodbye to his parents at the front door would be strange. He felt it would upset the whole trip. He wondered whether that was the reason he asked.

"Is that the sort of man I am?" he questioned himself. "If so, I am much too sentimental." But his desire to keep the familiar traditions of home unchanged was genuine. If not himself here, where else could he be that? As for his mother's affections, outgrowing them was something he could not fathom.

Jane observed her son deep in thought. With age, she felt he would become more of his father's son. Like his father, he too was taciturn. Unfortunately for Jane, her husband, not the most loquacious of men, was of little use when her deepest concerns needed airing. On these occasions she often turned to Monique.

Richard pleading, "don't you worry, Jane," in response to her, was a line so worn that she ground her teeth every time she heard it now. Only last week her dentist made her one of those teeth guards under the misconception that she ground her teeth in her sleep.

"Well, perhaps I am overstating the matter," she thought looking in Richard's direction. "Could be that I grind my teeth while asleep."

Gripped by a fatigue impossible to ignore, she heaved herself to her feet. Going to bed could no longer be held off. "Is it four o'clock then, Alex?"

"Yes," he replied as he and his father stood up.

"I will see you before then. Good night, son," she bade him softly. Alex moved toward her to have his cheek kissed; she obliged, and he embraced her.

"See you in a bit," Richard said and hugged her in turn.

"Good night, darling," she said as she turned to leave.

8. *The perfect family*

On the day after the party, as those who had attended went about their morning business, they could not help but smile, while reliving the many happy hours they had spent at Oak Leaf Farm.

Driving to school that Monday morning, Sarah Clark thought about the Hartley children: "No, they weren't any trouble. No one in Pinewood can remember them engaging in behaviour that was in any way untoward."

Driving past their house, she pondered: "How come they are so good at everything? It's uncanny." This was the very question she had posed marvelling at their results from the tests home-schooled kids took when joining formal education. Observing them closely during the year she taught them, apart from seeking permission to leave early on account of something benign, like a tummy ache, the Hartley kids were exemplary.

Remembering the trouble her own daughters caused her, she grimaced, stretching her lips into a thin line. How her girls would manage their studies without her there to push them, she simply did not know.

To distract herself from thoughts of her daughters, she more or less deemed it abnormal for children to behave and perform as well as the Hartley kids had. Alex was a doctor in the navy, Katherine a lawyer and Peter a marine biologist. Though grown and much changed now, their good manner and charm was undiminished, the very qualities that in the end had endeared them to her. At the party, she was genuinely pleased to see them and, watching them help their parents entertain, she was in no doubt that their parents were very proud.

"Are they the proverbial perfect family?" she mused, looking behind as her glance caught the roof of their house above the tree line. Momentarily, a streak of meanness overcame her, prompting her to comment: "God has a way of keeping us humble. They are almost the perfect family; almost, but not quite." The thought had her smirking all the way to school.

PART II

9. *Arendal*

On the last Sunday of September, at eight o'clock in the evening, Peter sat on a seafront bench in the small town of Arendal, in southern Norway. Around him, nature's preparation for winter was well underway. A cold wind from the sea nipping at his cheeks made him shift his head and burrow his hands deeper into his coat pockets. His averted gaze fell on a bronze statue of a woman seated on a plinth next to the bench.   Though the townsfolk didn't see fit to clothe her, she was not in disgrace; she held her head high, her mammæ pert and her childbearing hips generous. Unlike Peter, she did not avert her gaze but stared blithely out to sea. Behind her, lit up by a streetlamp, the yellowing leaves of a slender birch tree danced eagerly in the wind. Beyond the tree loomed the building occupied by his new employer where, early the next morning, he would report for work.

"Can't believe I am here at last," he whispered, happily breathing in the sea air. "Was it by coincidence, fate or providence?" he then wondered. But in the grand scheme of things he did not think it mattered one bit what you called it. And, that said, he was often surprised at how events in life were determined, how decisions made on seemingly small or trivial matters could cause such upheaval. What mattered more? The disruption occurring or that you had made the most of it?

"Isn't it fascinating how the mind is prone to recollect?" he mused with awe. "How it connects the dots and arouses one's curiosity?" Many years prior to stumbling across the job advertisement that had brought him here now, an article he had read stuck with him. In the northern part of Norway, on an island perpetually covered in permafrost, the article stated, a facility to store the planet's seeds had been constructed. It was to be a veritable Noah's ark for the preservation of seeds, an ark to secure earth's crop future in case disaster struck. It was situated deep in a mountain at an elevation high enough to keep its contents dry even if the ice caps melted. The temperature estimated by scientists, to rise no higher than minus three degrees, despite the predicted increased greenhouse effect, it was the perfect location. Moved by the article, he had applauded the forward-looking and pragmatic initiative. On seeing the job advertisement, his memory was jogged and his decision to apply as good as made. After all, what would it hurt to work with like-minded people? As for their desire to recruit someone with the courage of their convictions, he was without question the marine biologist they required.

Acquainted with no one in that part of the world and with little expectation of actually succeeding, he had nonetheless applied. But for the world converging, he would have been quite right. As it happened, someone had heard of him, and more to the point, learned about his professional work with dead zones. Peter had spent years researching dead zones for his doctoral thesis, for which he had garnered much praise. Though the topic was chosen foremost out of personal interest, it overlapped nicely with his sense of duty; a solemn civic duty as a citizen of planet Earth.

Inhabiting a world with much as yet to be ascertained, often he could not help but wonder if he had made the most of a situation. In any matter worth it's while, experience had taught him that self-doubt was always nearby. Making the most of opportunity was easier said than done and nothing was ever cut and dried. For Peter, questioning one's decisions was the true hardship in life. Reprising earlier thoughts, he determined that being prepared for any eventuality was far and away the best strategy. Merely putting out fires, already lit, was to his mind fraught with mediocrity. One must reach for a higher purpose! Did he not owe it to himself, to those who had come before, and to those yet to come? A fire once lit would only spread, becoming ever more difficult to extinguish.

Braving the wind, he turned to look at the sea, permitting his eyes to move further afield to the pier and on to the illuminated water beyond. The water swayed and bobbed its appeal to him, and although it was too cold to swim, the prospect excited him. He stood up and walked along the pier to the water's edge, the thought of swimming ever more tempting.

Staring at the water, he remembered the prediction made by fellow scientists that, as the ocean temperatures rose, warm water fish species would gradually make their way north. But in all the years he had tagged sharks, they had not made it this far.

Across the water, the homes on an island flickered their lights at him from their random altitudes on the hills. A boat from the island was headed his way and he noticed a small station tucked into a corner of the pier. Not having seen a bus come this way, he surmised that the boat was a ferry for local passengers, thinking: "That is what the station is for," as he looked at the small structure, partially sheltered from the wind by a glass wall. He supposed the two women deep in conversation who were presently seated there, were waiting for the ferry. His inability to understand them felt strange. Before his departure, with much concern for his welfare, his mother had asked how he could possibly work in

Norway when he did not speak the language. His patient answer had been, "true, Mother, but the majority of Norwegians do speak English."

Before reaching the harbour, the ferry slowed down, turned and came to a stop. There was only the skipper on board, and he greeted the women cheerfully as they boarded, revved the engine and set off again. With the distance growing, the people on board disappeared from sight and soon the ferry too, leaving only barely perceptible lights in its wake.

Deciding to go home, he turned his back on the sea and walked towards the centre of the town. As he walked, it struck him that he had used the word 'home' in reference to his apartment; he chuckled. Up until now, the only place he ever called home was the home of his childhood, Pinewood in North Carolina, not far from Chapel Ridge, where his parents lived.

"Yes," he thought, "this is to be home now," deciding that what he was undertaking would be considered growing up.

"To forsake the comfort and familiarity of home, instead, to relocate to a job and accommodations of one's own. That must be it!"

To his dismay, it dawned on him that though this was to be home, nothing here was familiar. The people were strangers, the streets foreign and his apartment above the shopping mall had yet to acquire the comfort and warmth of a home. Home, he believed, ought to be familiar and boast the feel of a worn but dear piece of clothing; the kind to make Saturday and Sunday mornings acquire that cosy, laid back sensation, a feeling replete with ease. At the very least, home was where loved ones resided.

"I am sticking out like a sore thumb here," he flustered, as his tally of the miles between him and those he loved, rose menacingly high. And the thought of his brother, sister and parents so far away tugged at something deep within his chest, causing tears to spring from his eyes. Blinking furiously to banish the tears that threatened to spill over, his reaction puzzled him. Why, the choice to move here had been entirely his own! His mother had been keen to spare him this quandary. This awareness did not make it any easier. Wishing to stay strong and not fall prey to his mother's doubts, he worked on dismissing them, only to discover he had his own doubts to contend with. "This is ridiculous," he thought, feeling he was letting the side down. Forlorn, he slumped in dejection and no longer felt as gallant as he had when he set out.

Going past a little public garden engulfed in darkness, a woman walking towards him suddenly crossed the street to avoid passing him. He wondered why no one thought to light it up. "Perhaps no one, except those intimidated by it at night notice," and contemplated whether, in time, when the streets became familiar, he too, might not notice how dark the garden was at night. But he recognised this wishful thinking. His life was such that, even if he treaded the same path daily, he would still perceive it and everything around.

Annoyance suddenly erupted in him at the thought of people treating familiarity with contempt. "Why are people so easily corrupted?" he muttered. How could they lose their sense of wonder when they so clearly needed it to inspire their duty as Earth's custodians? One would have thought they would cling to it for dear life.

"Is there a commission that gives greater meaning than the one to preserve life?" he questioned softly while looking pained. "And to keep me afloat?"

Recognising he was at risk he braced himself, took a deep breath and focused his mind to deny the turmoil lurking within. He must gain control and calm himself!

At top of his thoughts lay the recognition that any venture worth pursuing demanded sacrifice on the part of those who ventured out. He quickened his pace, while breathing deeply into his diaphragm, conscious to empty his lungs slowly but fully.

He walked briskly past the cinema. Earlier in the day, he had noticed that some of the buildings in town could do with a fresh lick of paint, especially the dated wooden ones by the seafront exposed to the elements. That said, he found them charming and felt that they added interest to the town. As far as small towns went, Arendal was decent enough. "I can live here quite well," he ascertained. It would by no means be like home, but then, that wasn't the point; flying the nest he understood would be all about finding one's own way.

Seeking out the bright side to life, in the manner he was conditioned to, he considered his apartment just about adequate for his needs. Trying a bit harder, he pinpointed something to actually love about the place; its location. It would take him all of three minutes to walk to his office, his shortest and greenest of commutes.

The sudden and loud clanging of church bells startled him as he crossed the street. He had learned that they belonged to the towering, red-steepled Catholic Church near the office. A bit of trivial information came to mind then, "Catholics and Anglicans have bell-ringing in common. And, so they should," he thought with a smile.

10. The foundation

Woken at seven by his telephone alarm, Peter dragged himself out of bed and into the bathroom. He felt out of sorts, "no one is immune," he thought sullenly, his disposition greatly compromised by jet lag. Turning on the shower without paying heed, he jumped when icy cold water splattered him. "Just what I need to wake up," he quipped, searching for his good nature. Adjusting the tap while avoiding the cold water, he stepped under the shower when the water warmed up. Soaking his body thoroughly, he reached for the shampoo, got a dollop, and proceeded to lather and scrub his abundant locks. Rinsing until his hair was free of lather, he then applied a generous amount of conditioner.

Remembering that he was in a hurry, he rinsed his hair again and hurriedly washed the rest of his body. Unable to resist, he swallowed a mouthful of water, gently arched his head backwards and let the warm water rain down his torso while it's soothing quality eased the strain in his shoulders and chest. Just before he got out, he swallowed even bigger mouthfuls and acknowledged that the water here tasted really good.

Wishing to arrive with time to spare, he dressed quickly, choosing his crisp new grey suit from Pierre, a blue shirt and a striped navy and ivory tie that his sister had slipped into his suitcase for just this occasion. "What a gem," he thought her, as his thumb and index finger ran along the length of the silk tie, which, oddly, looked rather familiar.

"Cheeky, isn't she?" he laughed quietly to himself. The tie was a grown-up version of his middle school tie. "How very like Kat," he uttered with affection. Draping it around his collar, he purposefully walked back to the bathroom and, while looking into the mirror, he fastened and tweaked until the tie was just right.

Scrutinising his image, he determined that he had too much hair. Katherine's advice to keep it long now felt somewhat dubious. Anyway, why should it matter to him if Alex had his hair tightly cropped? Though he longed to fit in with his new colleagues, he was never one to indulge his vanity. Reinforcement derived from clothing was not something he sought either. Knowing people as he did, however, he was aware that for many, clothing was the yardstick they used to take measure of others.

"Hard to believe, but there it is. Frivolous, aren't they?" he expressed to himself with disappointment. If it all boiled down to the piece of textile hanging on one's back, where did one's character fit in? But he knew this to be the way of the world. Had he not lived his whole life observing people and, more to the point, anticipating, sometimes rather anxiously, how they might behave around him? Observing individuals and society at large had become second nature and his judgements were rarely mistaken. In this case looking the part was key to quick assimilation into his new place of work and vital to his plans.

Walking into the kitchen for breakfast, he recalled his mother's clear instruction regarding food the evening before his departure and smiled: "Buy something unembellished, something in its natural state. *Real* food, Peter." He had lacked the heart to stop and remind her, that in all the years he had lived away from home he had steadfastly adhered to her advice. Instead, he had listened patiently as if it were the first time. And her influence now determined his breakfast; he boiled two eggs, paired them with steamed asparagus and fresh-brewed coffee from a small French press he had picked up at a store in town.

Eating alone, he had the company of his thoughts. Eager for the day, he permitted several scenarios of what might lie in store. He dwelled on the scenario of his ideal workplace – a very pleasant and stimulating place to work, with colleagues who were respectful, dedicated and hardworking. Committed to his cause, he was more than willing to stand up for his convictions and, if need be, fight for them. The excitement and eagerness he felt prior to leaving home was returning. Certain the night before was an anomaly, he couldn't wait to get started.

"This is more like it," he said, "I am a confident and dedicated scientist who is raring to go." He remembered Professor Jennings telling him that he was a stellar marine biologist. The compliment meant a great deal to him. The professor was one of the few people, Peter knew, who really understood how things were shaping up in the oceans and Peter had looked up to him.

His excitement grew and he was overwhelmed by it. "Uncanny," he murmured while cautioning himself to take it easy. "All in good time," but soon after this thought he cringed with unease. This phrase he felt, ought to be relegated to the past where it belonged, for there was no longer 'good time'. There was in fact no time to waste! Rising from the table, he quickly washed up and put everything away. He had lost track of the time and would now have to hurry. The clock never stopped ticking.

Grabbing his bag in the hallway he thought: "And now, finally, my chance to make a difference." He walked out to the stirrings of a September morning and to a rising sun that lit up his surroundings but added deceptively little heat. A faint breeze, too, from the sea met him, bringing with it a mild scent of the ocean and a chill that made him glad he was wearing his new cashmere suit.

At a quarter to eight, Peter nimbly walked into the lobby of North Marine Foundation. At the attendant's desk, Peter introduced himself and shook hands with the young man he recognised as Klaus. "It pays to do one's homework," he thought with satisfaction. Acquainting himself with his colleagues beforehand, he had read their biographies on the foundation's website. As a result, he was confident he could address everyone by name. Offering him a seat, Klaus reached for the telephone saying, "I will tell Lina you are here." Then Klaus walked over to take his photograph, explaining that it was for his employee identity card.

The Human Resource Manager, Lina, soon joined them. Bidding Peter good morning, she beckoned him to follow her to his new office. Listening to her speak, Peter thought she sounded just as she had during his Skype interview two months ago. Even now, when it was just the two of them, she was frugal, almost austere, with her words. Despite this quality, she had been the most stringent when pressing him on how firmly he held his convictions.

"I must have been convincing," he thought looking at her heavy frame amble down the corridor towards his new office. From the moment he stepped in, he was smitten by the expansive view of the sea. Since Lina only had business in mind, Peter got less than a minute at the window. When they were both seated, she clinically went through the personnel policy, highlighting the seven-and-a-half-hour workday and the foundation's flexible working hours scheme. He was at liberty to pick his own working hours, accruing a defined amount of credit and debit hours with the option to take time-off as flexi-leave. Lina proudly pointed out her finding that the scheme had substantially boosted productivity. That said, attendance at staff meetings was compulsory. He was entitled to six weeks of vacation in a year and, in accordance with Norwegian law, a minimum of three-months paternity leave.

Then she tackled the subject of remuneration, after which she gave Peter the opportunity to ask for clarity on matters discussed. But Jan from IT now stood at the door, signalling his turn.

"Alright, this should be sufficient to get you started. We'll cover the rest soon enough." Lina stood up, "I'll see you a bit later," she said and left. It now fell to Jan to acquaint him with their IT system, data policy and productivity tools. Lina came back with his identity and access card and put it on his desk without interrupting them.

Ten o'clock found Peter standing beside his boss, Stein Dale, and before his colleagues in the conference room as he waited to be presented. His introduction was to be a stand-up meeting, the sort of affair calculated to be short and crisp for everyone, no doubt, had more important things to attend to. Fixed in front of the entire staff left Peter flushing; he wasn't exactly keen on being the centre of attention. He hoped no one would notice. Unobtrusively, his eyes wandered around the room, taking in his new colleagues. The world was well represented here with staff hailing from all corners of the globe. Though quite aware of, indeed attracted by the foundation's cosmopolitan character, it was still exciting to behold. The group was small, consisting of twenty-five staff members. The beauty of a small establishment lay in its potential to be agile and cohesive, which, to Peter's mind, was a very good place to begin.

Feeling himself overdressed, he was self-conscious and wondered how he had missed that cue. His colleagues, by contrast, wore their Saturday and Sunday clothing, utterly casual, clearly wishing to extend the comfort of home into the workplace. Earlier that morning his choice of a suit had seemed to him a safe bet and he had reflected: "You can't go wrong with a suit." But here, it seemed he had. Mortified, he hoped they would not hold it against him.

"That's the problem with being interviewed on Skype; there isn't much scope to nail down the dress culture on the other end, especially when the interviewer's video conference system malfunctions," he determined. Then he remembered their website and recalled that most wore suits in the photographs there. Suddenly, his boss began to speak. Peter swiftly returned to the present and lent him his ear.

"Dear colleagues, allow me to extend a warm welcome to Mr Peter Hartley, our new marine biologist. Peter will be the head of the marine project on dead zones and it gives me great pleasure to welcome him to our organisation."

Turning to address him, Stein Dale continued: "Peter, we are very excited to have you here and we can't wait to get started. I'm confident your contribution will further our cause, strengthen our effectiveness, and in turn assist those we serve make decisions that will sustain our planet.

Our mandate is clear: we are to identify solutions that help reverse the substantial degradation of our oceans. Now, more than ever, policymakers around the world need to enact enlightened laws and fund measures to clean up the environment. On a personal note I have looked forward to discovering the ways in which we can complement each other, to make for a very fruitful working relationship. Welcome to our foundation Peter."

There was a warm round of applause for him. Though unexpected, he bore it well. And suddenly, a need to rise to the occasion seized him and he spoke: "My dear colleagues," he started, "human beings are not indispensable to the planet we call home. In fact, Earth would be better off without us – without our undue influence and interference. Rather than preserving her treasures, our ideals are wreaking havoc. Earth is being systemically poisoned. But then you already know that, and I suspect, it's the reason you have all found your way here."

Gauging his audience's mood and sensing they were receptive, he continued. "I am very pleased to make your acquaintance and look forward to working with all of you. I feel honoured to be here, to be a part of the team. The Earth consists mostly of water and all of her oceans are suffering; acidity levels and temperatures have increased treacherously these past years, causing untold damage. And we don't yet understand the full extent of this harm, or its implications, do we? But still, humankind continues to inundate our oceans with enormous amounts of carbon dioxide, nitrates leached from fields, sewage and the chemical run-off from the manufacturing industry. We are losing coral reefs and species whose existence depends on them at alarming rates. Most of the Atlantic Ocean between North America and Europe now lies in a zone with a very high PH balance. The Baltic Sea has dead zones. And there is, too, the growing problem of plastic pollution in the ocean, whereby millions of tons of plastic have a deadly effect on marine species and habitat. But are we to give up hope? Are we to let the die fall where they may? No! This is home. Let's not, therefore, continue to bite chunks out of the planet that sustains us. That is the height of foolishness. We'll only be shooting ourselves in the foot by such action. I am sure you will all agree with me when I say that being complacent is not something we can afford, not now, with the stakes as high as they are. My hope is that, together, we succeed in finding measures and solutions that will help reverse the trends that are poisoning our planet and, in turn, all of us. Let me not preach to the converted. I am touched by your warm welcome. Thank you very much."

After that, there were a lot of hands to shake and since etiquette demanded it, many eyes to look into as well. It was the polite thing to do when presented to someone, after all, and Peter relished the opportunity to search all eyes.

Since eyes were supposed to be windows to the soul, "I would save myself a lot of trouble if I could pick out the bad nuts now," he thought, partly in jest. Really, he was most interested in their eyes. His search was only skin-deep, and yet it was disappointing; the eyes he gazed into were as ordinary as they came.

11.   Under the boss's wing

At eleven o'clock on a Wednesday morning, during his third week at the foundation, Peter tapped on the doorframe of his boss' office. Stein, with whom he was now on first-name terms, looked up from his desk, "good morning, Peter. Come in and have a seat," he said smiling warmly.

Graciously, "good morning, Stein," Peter replied as he sat down.

Hoping to make the most of the meeting, he had prepared well. He had begun working in earnest on his core area of responsibility as soon as his contract had been signed by doing what research he could from the outside. To his surprise and dismay, however, the internal project documentation he now had access to was far less substantial than he had expected, and of dubious quality. According to the fairly superficial reporting available, actual progress was scant. Considering how little had been accomplished mid-way through the four-year implementation period, Peter's initial reaction was to start afresh.

The project folder contained nothing resembling an implementation plan; no detailed description of activities, deliverables or milestones and, likewise, no realistic budget. It seemed that the foundation's staff had more or less made things up as they went along. A practical tool framework for understanding whether the project was actually making progress in achieving its aims had yet to be developed. The scope of the existing project was very ambitious, however, making re-design a daunting task. He had never experienced such careless planning and preparation and wondered how it had ever been allowed to get this far. All this, lead him to believe that starting afresh, was the best option.

Stein, with concern asked, "how are you settling in?"

"Very well, actually. My workplace, supermarket and bank are just a few minutes away from my apartment," Peter responded in small talk, aware this was a fairly common indulgence when getting acquainted with someone. It was called breaking the ice. "What a strange saying. How do such sayings come about anyway?" he wondered as his mind went off at a tangent and began to contemplate the precarious state of the Arctic ice fields. He became aware of the frown encroaching on his countenance and quickly nipped it in the bud as he thought to himself: "What the world's ice needed was in fact the very opposite of breaking."

"Indeed, my wife and I love Arendal."

Peter listened attentively.

"The summers are wonderful here; we often spend them sailing in the archipelago. I feel quite at home."

"Are you not from here then?"

"Oh no, I am from Oslo, but my wife was born and raised in Arendal. She's the reason we moved, and I must say, it was a very good decision."

"Yes," Peter thought, "you do seem content."

"How's the team been treating you?" Stein asked laughing.

Peter chuckled knowingly. Stein was making light of his assimilation into the workplace. "Hard to say. I think you should ask me again in a month's time," he quipped.

"I will, but please remember that you can come to me at any time. My door, as you can see, is never closed." And this said, in a good-natured manner that touched Peter.

He had noticed that Stein's door was never closed, not even when he held meetings. "Open door policy," he said smiling, "how very modern and commendable." A sense of reassurance suddenly welled up inside him. Quickly catching hold of himself, he reined the emotion in. On account of people being such finicky creatures, it would not do to lay one's cards on the table.

Anyway, this was no time to be soft. His ambitions needed achieving and for him to succeed, obtaining Stein's approval for the entirely new project he had designed was crucial. And now, more than ever, he needed his wits about him and his best foot forward. He thought it most advantageous to prioritise certain aspects of the work; aspects that could easily be built on, that was. Once given the green light, he was confident it would be plain sailing from there on. Working on solutions to reverse degradation in dead zones was by no means new to him; he was an experienced hand. The main difference would be the temperature of the water. He had not before worked in waters this cold, but the prospect excited him.

In detail now, he described the project to Stein from his perspective. His experience with dead zones was extensive and, though he had worked mostly in the Gulf of Mexico, he was certain there was common ground and for something to be made out, on the question of reversing the degradation in dead zones, he believed it imperative that every aspect at play here be properly understood, first in isolation, and then as part of the whole. With some data from the Baltic Sea available at the Sea Institute in Grimstad, he explained, his analysis could commence immediately. This would enable him to draft a detailed plan for implementation. In terms of motivating the staff, he thought a phased approach to the work with triggers and milestones would be the best approach. To achieve momentum, it was important that the scientists keep to a clear schedule for their activities and deliverables so that they regularly had something to show for their efforts. Scientific analysis was challenging enough as it was, but phasing and organising the work into smaller, manageable tasks would hopefully boost morale among both the staff and the foundations implementing partners. He felt sure the work for the first phase was within budget and he hoped to stretch limited resources to accommodate several field visits for this initial stage.

"Peter, you have such compelling ideas. It's excellent work."

"Thank you, I sent a copy of the project document to you on Monday. What I discussed now is just an overview and it would be very helpful to receive feedback as soon as you are able. Then I can finalise the work plan." While he said this, it was not lost on him that his boss had not posed a single question to him.

"Yes, of course," Stein answered and, assuming a determined attitude, asked: "What do you know about green economy, Peter?"

The question surprised him, but he didn't give himself away. As it happened, his knowledge on the subject was honed. Peter made it his business to be well - informed on all matters pertaining to the environment and efforts to mitigate its degradation.

"I am well versed on the subject, as it happens," he answered, masking his perplexity.

"Good, in that case, you won't mind writing a small presentation for me. You see, I've been invited to a conference in Karlsruhe, Germany to give the key - note address; I'll need it by Monday morning. The conference begins on Tuesday, so we'll need to go through it together before I leave. Raising our profile at such events is important you understand, otherwise no one will take us seriously."

Peter was stumped for words; as well - informed as he might and should be, given his chosen profession, green economy was not his field of expertise.

Stein pushed a folder his way, "I have read your document. You are an excellent writer. These are the notes on the conference and some guidelines on the address I am to give. With writing skills such as yours, I am sure you will produce an outstanding presentation. If you have questions, I'll be here. Thank you, Peter. I am very grateful." And he rose to show him out the open door.

Peter walked to his office in a slight daze and slumped in his chair. Leaning his head back and closing his eyes he heard the low hum of his computer, as it beckoned. Thrown off by the turn of events, he was in no mood to pay that machine any heed. "What just happened in there?" he questioned himself. To say it was unexpected would be such an understatement. Key - note address, no less! He had no desire, in any shape or form, to write about green economy. This was not the reason for his being here. Besides, green economy wasn't in his job description or terms of reference. But then, he remembered something that made him sit right up. It was half a sentence tucked in at the end of one of the paragraphs describing his role. It had read ... 'and any other duties the Managing Director sees fit to assign.'

"He's got me on a technicality," he determined, annoyed he had allowed this to happen. Before signing his contract, he should have let Kat look at it. Little clauses, such as this one, were only meant to catch people out. He had let his guard down. And he wondered why he did, when dotting his i's and crossing his t's was such a vital part of protecting his personal business. Since the foundation didn't even have a specific mandate to work with green economy, he knew this would be a waste of his time. Looking at the clock about to strike noon, he decided on some air. Retrieving his jacket, he headed for the door and, passing Klaus in the lobby, he informed him he was going out to lunch.

Behind him Maiken said, "me too! Mind if I join you, Peter?"

"I'm going home, actually," he answered, knowing this response would put her off. The sting from the less than satisfactory meeting with his boss had left him poor company.

"Do you have food there?"

"Yes," he answered, unable to lie. Seeing the humour there, "how strange, she wants to eat my food. Is this going to be one of those days?" he wondered a little amused.

"Good, let's go then."

"Are you in the habit of inviting yourself to people's homes for lunch?" Peter asked miffed.

"Only those I work with," she grinned.

Since his remark was meant to offend, her answer surprised him.

"This one is intriguing," he thought to himself smiling.

"How was your meeting?"

"Not great. How did you know about that?"

"What did he think of your submission?" she asked ignoring his question.

"I didn't get any concrete feedback on it?"

"Do you think he understood what you told him?"

"What?" he asked in alarm.

"He doesn't really know much about the work we do."

"Maiken, what are you saying?"

"Just that; he doesn't quite grasp what we do here, or what we are supposed to be doing, anyway."

"Oh, dear God," he moaned.

With a knowing laugh, "what did he ask you to do for him?"

"Write a conference paper on green economy."

"Are you going to?"

"I am bound to do so by my contract, even though it's outside my field."

"He loves conferences," she stated, her eyes instantly ablaze with disdain. "See you back at the office. Just remembered something I must do."

"She did take offence," he determined as questions he would have liked to ask her, suddenly and voraciously cropped up in his head. And what did she mean by: "He doesn't really grasp the work we do?" Peter deliberated crestfallen. Looking at her, the manner of her walk gave away the knowledge that she knew he was watching. It was there in her bouncy step, in the slight skip in her feet as she picked them off the ground.

"But she still wants my attention," he gathered from her parading act.

Rendered thus unproductive by his disappointing meeting, Peter spent hours exploring sections of the coast he hadn't been to before. During this walk he grew anxious that his ambitions might well be under threat. Would his boss jeopardize his plans? If the man at the helm of an organisation was grossly incompetent, was there any reason for hope? He had learned, that politicians had appointed Stein and made sure his contract kept getting renewed. That's how it worked the world over, but here too? Going by Maiken's account, Stein was out of his depth, which only meant that those who had appointed him made little effort to ensure he would be an effective manager. So again, was there any hope he could fulfil his ambitions here if the man at the top lacked the ability and awareness to truly appreciate the importance of his work?

Seeking consolation, later that evening he called Katherine on Skype.

"Hi Kat."

"Peter! How are you?"

"Had a nasty surprise at the office today, a possible setback, and I'm calling to cry on your shoulder…if you'll let me."

"Anything for you. Please tell me."

"My boss may turn out to be a problem, an obstacle of sorts. Perhaps I'm overreacting…"

"What? Come on, stop joking."

"I regret signing my contract without consulting you first. Stein wants me to work on something outside my field. It is without question a diversion from my work Kat, but he's got me on a technicality. Have a look on page three; I'm sending the contract to you now."

"How much of your time does this work require?" Katherine asked, ever so practical.

"The rest of the week and the weekend if I am to do it justice."

"Well, that's not too bad, Pete. Be practical about this. Get it done and leave it behind you."

"I've thought about that, but I am afraid this is just the beginning, that this is how he operates."

"I just got it, let me see...."

Peter waited.

"I'm afraid you're right, he has you, so my advice is that you hunker down, punch that paper out and then avoid him like the plague. He might leave you alone after that and let you get on with your primary task."

"Is this your professional opinion?" Peter teased.

"Oh Pete, stop, take it easy. Hopefully it won't go that far."

"Don't worry Kat, I am capable of putting my foot down. I just needed some consolation. Have you seen mum and dad lately?"

"Yes, last weekend. They came to see my new house."

"Why didn't I hear about this?" he asked feeling left out and a little sad.

"You are the one who decided to leave, remember?" she challenged him.

He was not yet forgiven for leaving. "Kat, you know I miss you."

"Come and see the house then. I know you'll love it. It's on Windermere Peninsular and only three miles from the harbour, neatly perched on a hill, so I shan't worry about flooding...not for the time being anyway. It's a real find Pete, I feel so fortunate. Alex and I thought of having a pool in the basement. What do you think? He's around by the way, helping me manage the renovations."

Alex's face appeared on the screen then.

"Did she bully you into helping?" Peter asked laughing, knowing Alex was not immune to Kat's manipulations either.

"Not at all. Thankfully, there was none of that this time. Just thought I would keep an eye on her while she settles in. When she's done with the work, I'll spend the weekends at home. I like having mum and dad all to myself."

"Ah ... you wimp!" Peter said playfully, deflecting the jibe intended to rile him.

"You wouldn't be saying that if you were in the vicinity."

"How very unlike you to forget. Kat and I know everything you get up to, everything. You taught us remember?"

"By the way, I noticed you hadn't logged on in the last two days. I know you're busy Pete, but we need to be thorough. It's the only way we'll identify something we can work with. You also need to vary the times you log on. We must have a well-rounded picture. Remember we're aiming for intimate knowledge."

"I am sorry, I'll do better this week. Promise."

"The other reason for my being at Kat's is to discuss our observations thus far."

Peter bade his brother and sister goodnight and prepared for bed. Alex was right; he would spend more time observing from now on.

12.   Off course

Even at the best of times, waiting was difficult. In the week that Stein attended the Green Economy Conference in Karlsruhe, Germany, contrary to promise, Peter had not received any word from him. His patience was truly tried. All Peter required of him was the green light to proceed with his project. Why this proved so difficult for his boss was beyond comprehension. Twiddling one's thumbs was all well and good for an hour or two, but after a few days it became a source of annoyance. With the silence persisting, on Thursday, taking matters in hand, he decided to pay a visit to their partners at the Sea Institute in the neighbouring coastal town of Grimstad. Knowing the other team members, Amanda and Luke, were already well - acquainted with them, he declined their offer to accompany him. Their time would be better spent on more pressing matters. Besides, in his sullen state it was best that he be alone. Peter spent twenty of the thirty minutes of the bus ride elevating his mood and the last ten sightseeing as the bus drove across the town of Grimstad to the Sea Institute.

Apprehensive about the fairly short notice he had given Eric, his counterpart, at the Institute Peter presented himself to the receptionist rather timidly. "I believe Eric is expecting me. I'm Peter, by the way."

"He's on his way down," she said eyeing the double doors opposite her desk with expectation, then nodding, as they swung open to reveal Eric. Welcomed warmly, Peter was led to the offices and introduced there.

"Now that's done, I can show you the laboratories," Eric cheerfully said, intimating the best was yet to come.

Smitten by his enthusiasm, Peter said: "Lead on, I can barely wait." They walked up a flight of stairs and when Eric opened the door at the top, out of shear excitement, Peter nearly choked on his breath when he uttered; "look at that! Why aren't all laboratories built to benefit from natural light in this way?" The sunny, airy room was magnificent. Looking around he recognised at once that no expense had been spared on equipping these facilities. The microscopes were the best money could buy. From the workstations to the sturdy wooden floors, from the friendly floor plan to the ergonomic furniture, everything was spick and span, and all of it great, modern design. All this reminded Peter that he was in the richest country on Earth. This was definitely not your dingy laboratory tucked away in a basement somewhere. And his visit went swimmingly.

Just before he left, Peter was taken down to the harbour to see the two special-purpose boats used for the data collecting ventures at sea. While inspecting them, it dawned on him that he had not been on the water in more than a month and was tempted to ask Eric to take him out. Fearing that might be overstepping the mark, he resisted the urge.

He departed the Institute feeling uplifted. Sometimes getting away did the trick. It was all one needed. On the bus home, he deemed the Institute vital to his work. His opinion of their setup was favourable, and the partners were amiable. Since their data would be the basis for the first part of his analysis and reflection to determine a more specific direction for his project, he felt reassured. Working with reliable data in his field was everything. If he had a say in the matter, he would have preferred to collect all of his own data, but one was forced to collaborate and trust others.

To see for himself, however, he would propose accompanying Eric and his colleagues on some of their missions. Presenting the request, as simply a desire on his part to know his partners would be fine, he felt. He hoped they would not take offence. Remembering his far from adequate dealings with his boss, he was uncharacteristically uncertain how to proceed. Then, an idea occurred to him prompting the following mental note, "I should get some insight into the rules of conducting business here."

The following day, Peter arrived at work to find Stein chatting in the lobby with Klaus. Looking up to see who walked in, Stein beamed and extended his hand. "Peter, what an asset you are. Your presentation was very well received. It won me a place on the new advisory committee. Isn't that wonderful?"

Peter immediately saw where this was headed and felt himself recoil as he thought, "good news is it? But how can it be?" Though it was intended to, Stein's display of enthusiasm did not encourage him in the least. Was the presentation he wrote really that effective?

"Come to my office for a moment," Stein invited him cheerfully.

In the office, he poured them coffee.

"This is not at all spontaneous," Peter established. "It's been planned."

"This is a very good start for us, Peter," Stein said excitedly.

But which start exactly was in question here? Was Stein referring to Peter's start at the foundation or did he speak of his own with the green economy committee? If the latter, Peter was doomed. If the former, well... he was doomed then too, for he perceived that he had yet to begin.

"You should have been there with me, Peter. The excitement at the conference was overwhelming. We are definitely on to something here. Progress will come out of this; just you wait and see. Our next conference is in three months. Since I'm now on the committee, my responsibilities have grown substantially. Can I count on you Peter?" he asked, as his eyes bored into him with intensity.

Peter held his gaze but, within him, his spirit had withered a little. The start in question, as he had feared, was Stein's own little side - line; it had nothing to do with Peter's core task, much less with the organisation's mandate. "But to what end?" To distract him, he quickly managed, "I hope my project proposal, which I submitted to you last week, is of an equally high standard. Am I to progress as it stands, or do you see the need to make changes? You haven't yet provided any comments."

"Oh ...Yes," Stein smiled, "I will have an answer for you by the end of today."

"Thank you very much, Stein, that would be much appreciated." Peter rose abruptly, leaving before anything else could be said.

He was now convinced that the man would be difficult and was certainly not the type to listen. He would have things his own way! This behaviour must be what Maiken had tried to warn him about. Realising he had not spoken to her since, he made a beeline for her office and at her door paused to observe her. Sensing his presence, she swiftly turned to the door. Peter perceived fortitude in the manner she had abruptly turned.

"Hello there. I have plenty of food in my apartment. Care for some lunch?" he asked smiling.

"Actually, I'm very busy today," she curtly answered.

A smile broke out on his face as he detected her desire to make him beg. He obliged: "Please do come, Maiken. I am giving you plenty of notice, at least three hours. That's more than you gave me."

Waiting for her response, he thought, "I hope she comes. I'm desperate for information on that blind sordid man. Since she is the only one, to have indicated that the boss is inadequate, I must pursue the matter with her."

"If I say I am busy, it really means I am, Petter."

Maiken had mispronounced his name and he knew it was purposefully done.

He walked to her desk, leaned on it and facing her squarely said: "My name is Peter, not Petter."

"Does it matter?" she challenged.

"Oh yes, my mother would definitely think so. She chose it for me, you see."

"I will have dinner with you tonight if you like, Peter."

"She is as bad as Katfish," he assessed unable to hide the grin that usually accompanied the thought or use of his sister's pet name.

"Meet me at the post office. Six o'clock sharp."

"Six o'clock, and don't be late!" he warned as he left.

13.   Maiken

Afraid Maiken might leave if she arrived before he did, Peter was early. Besides, the thought of a woman waiting alone in the dark was disquieting. November days this far north were all too dark. Though not yet six, in the evening, the sun set several hours ago. In the morning, his walk to work was in the dark and so was his return.

Thinking about the office reminded him that Stein had left for the day without giving him the promised feedback. As things stood, he would have nothing to work on all weekend, delaying his start even further. Since his heart was set on this project, the stalling and deviation was maddening. Sturdily leaning against the post office wall, he waited patiently, as he had these last fifteen minutes.

She arrived on the dot at six. Delighted to see her, his greeting was a relieved, "nice to see you!"

She smiled in response and briskly asked if he had a place in mind.

Perceiving this a very good start, he replied eagerly, "I read about the new restaurant and I'm hoping you haven't been yet. Shall we try it? It's only a minute or two from here, down by the harbour."

"Yes, why not, sounds great," she replied.

Making conversation as they walked, Peter asked if she had heard anything about the restaurant.

"No, but I'm sure we'll soon find out."

"Well, the review I read online was quite positive," he told her reassuringly.

Having observed the grin he had quickly suppressed, she said, "what?"

"Actually, the google translation I read was rather crazy, but I got the gist of it."

"It would really have killed you to ask for help, right?" she teased. But Peter heard the tension in her laughter and sensed her guard was firmly in place. Unfortunate, he thought, that such tension should exist between the sexes as they became acquainted. Maiken needed not fear him.

"The name is Hartley," Peter said to the host at the restaurant when they arrived. "We have a reservation for two." A surprised Maiken gaped at him and when he playfully winked at her, she laughed once again. Her laughter, in this instance, sounded as though she was freeing herself from all trouble and, for the moment, rendered joyful and uninhibited. Wishing he could laugh as easily, Peter looked on with envy.

When Maiken took off her long coat, Peter saw that she wore a dress. "The creature has legs!" he observed admiringly as she handed her coat to their host. Caught off-guard, he forgot to hand over his own overcoat. A slight throat clearing from their bemused host soon returned him to his senses as he self-consciously surrendered the apparel. Though merited, he resisted the urge to pay her a compliment. In all respects, this was a business meeting; one that he hoped would help him make sense of his boss and the lie of the land. And the land in question was of course, the office…its leadership, the organisational culture and all other important aspects. His feelers, so to speak, would be sent probing until he was satisfied.

Once seated, a waiter eager to impress them appeared with the menus and, in no time, their drinks. Their orders taken, the guests at table two not yet properly acquainted eyed each other speculatively.

"Here's something to interest you," Maiken declared with a hint of mischief. "Two summers ago, someone saw a shark in the Norwegian Sea. Specifically, a great white from the tropics."

"No, you don't say!" he blurted out, as excited by this surprising story as he was by her neglect of small talk.

"It's true," she insisted. "I remember that summer well. July had temperatures in the mid-twenties, with clear blue skies. There was so little rainfall that all the berries in the forest shrivelled up and dropped from their bushes. There was no berry picking that summer."

Barely containing himself, Peter eagerly leaned forward as his eyes implored her to elaborate. "What a stunning development," he exclaimed.

"Yes, isn't it just," she affirmed.

"It's already happening," he mumbled under his breath, attempting to come to grips with the news. He believed her and though expected, it was still something he had to digest.

Permitting him no time, "are you aware that the cod in the Atlantic can barely keep up with the plankton now?" she continued. "With the warming of the water, the plankton easily outruns the cod. The fluidness of warm water is apparently easier to traverse than colder water. Before the warming, the density of the water was for them similar to that of maple syrup, so that movement in this colder water was much more demanding on their part. The speed at which they can now move in the warmer water has more than tripled. As a result, the cod don't get enough to eat, nowhere near enough, as to enable them to reproduce like before."

"An excess amount of food, or the lack of it, is known to bring about modification in living organisms. Many naturalists subscribe to this principle ... as do I," Peter stated. "I hope it won't lead to extinction for the cod. They must adapt quickly. And, as if that is not challenging enough, the poor fish also have to contend with plastic contamination."

"Plastic, sadly, is not food," Maiken protested.

"I know, but food is taking on new meaning in our time, is it not? There is a new dimension to it; the poisoning of consumers." Suddenly, remembering alarming news he had read about Sweden, he piped out: "Did you know that jellyfish once clogged up the water pipes to a Swedish nuclear power plant?"

"No! I didn't. Anyway, how would *you* know that? I'm the one who lives in Scandinavia."

"The jelly fish in the Baltic Sea are transforming into giants," Peter calmly stated, as he thought of the menace they were fast becoming, not only in the Baltic Sea, but the Gulf of Mexico and all along the Japanese coastline. Some of them now weighed as much as a hundred and fifty kilograms. Jellyfish were a resilient fish capable of regeneration and some species were known to live forever. They could even survive in dead zones.

"Fortunately, the nuclear plant had an alternative inland water source," he noted solemnly, thinking now about all the developments that captivated him, as he decided to share something else and this time, something to do with human beings. "Have you heard about the Spanish family that cannot feel pain?"

"No, I haven't," Maiken replied, shaking her head in disbelief.

"A mother passed the gene to her daughter who, in turn, bequeathed it to her son. That's three generations. The boy once broke his leg and felt no pain. I think that's amazing! I find the fact that the gene is transferable to both sexes very interesting. What on earth could be the cause of that? And that's not to mention those incredible siblings in Germany, who have reverted to walking on all fours."

His thoughts had now slipped into a familiar groove and passionately: "On the other side of the globe, in New Zealand, you have authorities in the city of Canterbury advising pregnant woman to test their drinking water for nitrates in order to prevent their babies from being born with the Blue Baby Syndrome. Their intensive cattle and dairy farms use nitrogen fertilisers to turn arid scrubland into high - yielding fodder fields. The nitrates from the fertilisers seep into the ground and inevitably find their way to the rivers. And, so does the bovine dung and urine. With as much as six and a half million cattle living there, many rivers are no longer fit for swimming."

"Are your parents still together?" Maiken asked in a turnaround that dumbfounded him. Serenely she added: "My parents did not marry. They chose to live together, but not to tie the knot. To those who had cared to listen, they attested to their partnership being built on a foundation set in rock, with no sand in sight and therefore, needed not be concerned with the triviality of marriage, as they saw it. But, a few years down the road, about the time I turned eight, my father's commitment to mother waned. Eager for a fresh start, he left on the very day he disclosed his indifference. Most puzzling to me, was the fact that six months later he got married."

She shrugged her shoulders then and laughed with unease. "Everything happened very quickly. There was hardly any time for me to adjust to my new set of circumstances."

She fought to subdue her emotions. Peter felt her sadness and, sensing she had stopped talking, searched for consoling words.

But, to his surprise, she continued: "Not to be outdone, my mother married that year, too! Now I have four half-siblings and along the way I seem to have slipped through the cracks. I am the awkward spare child that doesn't quite fit in with either family."

Pressed now for something to say, "what's your opinion of the institution?" he blurted out. Only posed for the want of diversion, the question he realised was far from suitable.

"I know for certain that marriage is not for me. I plan on being a hermit," she said with spirit, as her eyes held his gaze and dared him to challenge her.

But she was wrong to expect a challenge from him on this count. Instead, her remark made him giddy. "Since she's disinclined to be involved or get hitched for that matter, I can be friends with her," he assured himself.

Presuming, therefore, that work would be preeminent in her life, he felt hopeful. Enquiring into the meaning of his newly found hope, he recoiled in an instant. "What if she is a marine biologist too? I am lonely and in untested waters." That, in his opinion, was somewhere he dared not go.

For propriety's sake, he told her his parent's story. "My parents have been together all their lives," he said, sounding to his own ear, strangely apologetic. "Well, nearly all their lives. They were childhood sweethearts who went to medical school together and married just after graduating. Due to mother's poor health they moved to America in search of a warmer climate. Her asthma was unmanageable in England." And dreamily, he added, "I can't imagine them apart."

"You really are very lucky," she cried.

Scrutinising her face and finding only candour there, "yes, I am," he agreed.

"I take it you did not inherit your mother's asthma."

"Thank goodness, no," he answered. "But I did inherit other qualities from her which, unfortunately, I'm not at liberty to discuss," he said with a playful grin.

"Why would you assume that I care?" she countered while thinking him a tease.

"Well, don't you?" he demanded pointedly.

Taken aback by his directness, she merely shook her head.

Peter could not believe she was at a loss for words. Seizing his chance, he offered, "I've wanted to ask you about Stein since we last spoke, since just after my meeting with him. You remember, don't you?"

"Is that what this is all about? You, getting the scoop from me?" she asked feeling her emotions stir.

"Yes, and you were the one to bring up the subject. On the day, I got the distinct impression there was something you wished to share with me. You said it yourself, he is clueless and not in the least helpful. And, though I know I've just arrived, but where is everyone, where does everybody go? There's ever only half the staff at the office as far as I can tell," he said, shaking his head in frustration. "One would think they worked elsewhere."

Prepared for him to deny his intention for meeting her, his sincerity disarmed her. Yes! She had been the one to broach the subject but, remembering his passionate address to them on his first day, she had regretted her action and no longer wished to be the one to tell him. It was only a matter of time anyway before he realised their predicament. As for the staff, they were in fact 'working elsewhere'; most of them were preoccupied with criss-crossing the globe to attend all kinds of seminars, conferences and workshops. Maiken had observed that only a fraction of these innumerable trips were either necessary or productive.

"Let's not talk about work, Peter. I'm afraid I'm not really in the right frame of mind for that kind of conversation," she appealed to him.

Acquiescing with some reservation, he masked his impatience and said gently, "alright, another time then."

Apologetic, she nodded.

Though he would depart none the wiser than when he arrived, he resigned himself to the fact and focused on enjoying her company. She was amiable now and the change was without question a result of his honesty. The vexing woman from before had disappeared and, in her place, sat a pleasant companion who delicately sipped her wine and conversed with charm, leaving him inclined to accommodate her talking whenever she liked and on any subject of her choosing.

Appetizing food was served and both of them eagerly turned to it. "How's your appetiser?" Peter asked politely.

"Delicious, very tasty," Maiken responded sweetly, though, she was annoyed with herself, for being soft on him. Though the perfect opportunity for a row had presented itself, she had simply let it go. If only he had not been so frustratingly forthright! His honesty had made any quarrel impossible. As far as she was concerned, the whole evening was a let -down. It hadn't at all gone according to plan. Why did she suddenly develop this infuriating need to protect him? Why protect him from being disillusioned when she herself suffered from it a great deal? Deep within, Maiken felt disadvantaged by her nurturing instinct, that inborn trait in females to nurture everyone, including grown men.

14. At loose ends

Peter whiled away his Saturday morning, drinking more coffee than was good for him. Being in no mood for observation, after a leisurely shower in the early afternoon, he decided to spend his time unpacking the rest of his belongings. Alex would not be pleased, but neither he nor Katherine suffered the same frustration he did at work. Apparently, his boss's word stood for very little; he had still not heard from Stein.

He was suddenly filled with envy for his sister, whose firm kept her busy. Though her colleagues were wary of involving her in their cases, plenty of paralegal work still ended up on her desk. Even so, newly employed as an environmental lawyer, Kat was impatient to be assigned her own cases and complained about how slowly she was being shown the ropes. Sometimes, she had told him, the senior lawyers asked her to get them coffee.

At the Warfare Command in Norfolk, Alex was a hero. All sorts of medals would soon be conferred on him for his bravery and competence. When his ship the USS Kaine collided with a cargo ship in Asia, early in spring, causing great damage to the hull that nearly sank the vessel, Alex had rescued many of his colleagues. After the accident, afraid he might be suffering from post-traumatic stress syndrome, his superiors referred him to a psychologist for evaluation. Even though he received a clean bill of health, he was sent home on summer leave a bit early. Peter and Katherine had rearranged their schedules to spend time with him. As soon as he got home, Peter had asked Alex if he was in fact traumatised.

Without hesitation he had answered, "yes, I am heartbroken but, not for the reasons my superiors think. You, of course, know better. I'm gutted that we lost so many. I tried to take them as quickly as possible to the surface, Pete, so they could breath. But they just couldn't hold out long enough. Despite all their training, they were still so vulnerable. On the day, it boiled down to the matter of biology, pure and simple. The saddest part was that not all bodies were found; we left my shipmates at sea."

Alex was now in charge of a new programme that would keep him at Naval Station Norfolk, in Virginia, for the foreseeable future. The programme was classified, but when Peter asked him about it, he gave the game away by letting slip, "do you remember the time you tagged sharks?"

Since Alex was in the navy, it stood to reason that he would be tagging human beings not fish. Knowing how shaken the Navy was by the recent ship collisions and fatalities, it was easy for Peter to deduce that his brother's new responsibilities had to do with safety. Alex's ship collision was the second in a span of less than a year. His brother's expertise in diving medicine, a specialisation unto its own, only reinforced his reasoning.

Desiring better comfort in his home, Peter went to the guest bedroom to determine how involved the task of unpacking his books would be. He felt the moment opportune since his Christmas holiday would be spent at his granny's in Yorkshire. "Something good might as well come of this downtime," he muttered to himself as he moved to the living room and wondered whether he was pleased with the placement of the bookshelves. Once filled, it would be a bigger chore to move them, "and perhaps I might not have the time," he thought wistfully, hoping he would be immersed in work by then.

With the sofa positioned in the only place it could possibly fit, he saw that the bookcases would have to stay where they were. One creature comfort Peter truly appreciated was a sofa big enough to accommodate his long frame. Surely no other repose would do for the reading of a favourite book in the comfort of such a sofa and finally dosing off.

Retrieving two boxes to start with, he spent the rest of the day reunited and reminiscing with his books.

On Sunday, the urge for a swim became irresistible. Taking the situation in hand, he searched online for a public pool, and found one only half-an-hour away by bus in the neighbouring municipality of Flomland. Upon arrival he was pleasantly surprised by the quality of the facilities, given that he seemed to find himself in a small community in the countryside. Here was a modern pool half the Olympic length, a large sauna, a spotless changing room outfitted with plenty of lockers, a spacious shower area and complete fitness facilities. Inspecting the pool more closely, he was ecstatic to discover that UV sanitising technology was used to clean the pool.

The lifeguards on duty during his swim were the most vigilant he had come across in ages. Part of him resented their alertness. In the absence of any enjoyment, he swam languidly and effortlessly under their watchful eye, for an hour.

Emerging finally from the pool, "that was really pleasant, thank you," he said to the young lifeguard.

"You are most welcome," she responded with a broad smile.

"You are the most attentive group of lifeguards I've encountered in a long, long time."

A shadow crossed her faced as she remarked: "A teenager drowned here not so long ago you see. He came here as a refugee to start a new life, and it ended in this spot, of all places, on our watch."

"Oh, I am very sorry," Peter consoled her, as his suspicion that their watchfulness went beyond the norm was confirmed. Being in the water was dangerous, life-threatening even, as the upsetting case in hand abundantly proved. He chastised himself for resenting their alertness.

"So am I," she said softly and looked away.

On the bus ride back to Arendal, Peter's mood was subdued as his mind drifted to his siblings. For him, swimming was intensely personal and an activity best indulged with his brother and sister. Without them, though enjoyable, it was not the same.

15. The chairman

In spite of the luxury he was afforded, comfort eluded Peter. Wishing to remove himself, his eyes escaped through the window to the picturesque winter. The beauty outside captivated him. The sun had cast its spell on the surrounding forest of native conifers. Heavy with snow, the branches of countless spruce, pine and birch trees bowed precariously. Peter watched as a worn branch let slip its load and the packed snow dropped to the white mounds beneath.

On the outskirts of Oslo, about a four-hour train ride north of Arendal, in a plush room with a fire blazing merrily in the hearth, the foundation's end-of-year board meeting was in session. Plastic water bottles – one of the West's trappings of affluence – were neatly arranged in front of each guest. Apart from him, everyone at the table seemed happy to drink the water essentially contained in an oil product. Though Peter could not relate, they all seemed at peace with the confounding habit.

Failing to come to terms with their blindness, he exclaimed within, "but these are educated people, who cannot be ignorant of the fact that oil is the raw material used to manufacture plastic! Could be that they perceive a magic membrane dividing the two," he devised, trying to make sense of this common madness.

He picked up a bottle and saw that the water would expire in six months. As far as he was concerned, the most important information was missing – how long the water had been in the bottle.

Most of the morning, he had watched in disbelief as the chairman presided over the meeting, in a manner he deemed inappropriate, to say the least. A manner that made certain from the very beginning that everyone present was in no doubt about who was in charge here. That fact in itself would have been unproblematic had his remarks not been curt, dismissive and derisive. In the hope of sparing themselves from the chairman's sharp tongue, most of the assembled board members studiously avoided eye contact. And yet their eyes betrayed distinct unease.

Present at the meeting were the six members of the board, two of them female, his boss Stein, the foundation's finance manager, Bjørn, and the staff representative, Elise. His own presence was by pure happenstance. In order to provide variation to the agenda, with only a day's notice, Peter had been invited to talk about his project, funding for which had finally been approved by the finance committee of the board.

As his gaze roved around the table for the umpteenth time, he saw that those seated around it pretended nothing here was amiss. "But what could possibly be more unappealing than a rude old privileged man?" he questioned himself. "If he cannot be civil or constructive, why is he even here? Why is he *still* on the board at all?" Sadly, Peter was in no doubt it was the chairman's uncouth mouth and sharp elbows that kept him in this position. The man, as far as he could see had mediocre qualities and his bullying behaviour was untoward. Experience had taught Peter, that this sort of mediocrity only thrived in a malfunctioning system.

Elise was called upon to speak and Peter, having now experienced the board atmosphere, braced himself. Their colleagues in Arendal, who had helped Elise prepare for just this opportunity, were hoping for a positive outcome.

"I am here to speak on behalf of the staff," Elise began as she took the floor. Her eyes darted around the table with apprehension, her discomfort obvious. "There is near consensus among the staff members that the foundation suffers from a chronic lack of leadership, managerial competence and strategic vision. This impinges on the foundation's operational effectiveness while severely undermining staff morale and productivity. Our strategy was last updated eight years ago and we are lagging behind. Recent discoveries in our field of expertise have exposed that our efforts have been outpaced and that our relevance, indeed our very mandate is under question. The degradation of the environment is more advanced than was thought. The past four annual staff assessments – all of which were submitted to the board – have revealed that confidence in management has steadily deteriorated. As we are funded by taxpayer money, accountability is paramount. But poor management has compromised the foundation's ability to be fully accountable for its resources and results. All of this information is clearly presented in the staff report before you. I hope all the board members have taken the time to study the report and consider our recommendations."

"Elise," the chairman suddenly barked, "I hear your complaint. But why have you been stirring things up among the staff?"

Despite being witness to the morning's proceedings, and countless others before then, Elise was stunned by this attack.

"But I am not stirring up the staff! As their elected representative, I'm merely articulating their concerns as faithfully as I can," she protested, with as much poise as she could muster.

"This assessment is your own, isn't it? You are the sole author."

"My own assessment?" she asked uncomprehending his outrageous accusation.

"Yes, and you can stop being coy about it: Your behaviour is simply unacceptable for a staff representative."

"I sent copies of the questionnaires filled out by the staff in their own free hand, to each board member seated at this table. This is not *my* assessment and I have not in any way misused the process or my position," she said failing miserably at being assertive.

"Elise, you are mistaken if you think I will allow dissent from a smattering of disgruntled, incompetent staff. I suggest you speak to Stein when you get back to Arendal and sort out these grievances directly with him. I am aware of his open-door policy."

Elise began to lose her composure and stared at the chairman in disbelief. "This is not about me," she said choking back her humiliation and her tears.

Peter looked at his boss, who though clearly embarrassed by Elise's revelations... recognised he would not be undone by the damning report at this meeting. His sudden beaming gave him away. The chairman had given Stein his seal of approval. Poor Elise was denied the chance to properly state her case on behalf of those she represented, the staff; the lifeblood of the foundation.

Not quite finished with her yet, Nesheim pressed on: "Spare us the emotion, will you, please. And when you talk to Stein, may I suggest you pick a time when you are less excited. Your discussion might be more productive then," he added, squaring the full force of his intimidating glance on her.

A practiced hand at abasing people, he took one look at Elise, now a quivering mess, sure in the notion that none of this would reflect poorly on him. When had it ever had consequences for him anyway? And, in her state, with tears running down her face, how could it not be her fault? Her conduct was unprofessional. This was a boardroom and no place to wear one's emotions on one's sleeves.

The chairman had turned the tables on the staff representative with impunity. Their dissatisfaction with the management of the foundation would simply be ignored, and not for the first time. It was not lost on Peter that, though they may have felt uncomfortable with the situation, none of the participants had so much as attempted to intervene or engage the discussion in any way, much less take any action to defend Elise.

Determined to neutralize the palpable tension in the room, Mr Nesheim briskly proceeded to the next agenda item and, turning to Peter, declared casually, "I believe you have something to present to the board."

"May I say, Sir, before I commence, that in our field of work, emotion is rarely misplaced. In my opinion, a good dose of passion would do us all a world of good."

"Young man, we have no time for your philosophising. Start your presentation."

Peter had taken a chance, and this response did not surprise. As he walked to the podium, it was plain he had offended the chairman. Recognizing him as the kind of man to lash out at people when questioned or challenged, he knew it would not be long before he himself became a target.

"The oceans..." Peter commenced.

"Look at the clock ladies and gentlemen. Why, it's time for lunch," Mr Nesheim interrupted, pushing his chair outwards and abruptly rising from it. The sound of chairs scraping the floor as others followed suit to leave for the adjoining dining room filled the room.

Peter looked on aghast. "Here it is," he thought, "and he didn't keep me in suspense for long." He was right about him, though his insight bestowed no gratification. In this instance, being proven wrong would have been better. Contemplating why he had been asked to begin if short on time, the answer came easily: "In order to humiliate me." Coming to Elise's defence in the man's eyes was a faux pas. To avoid mutiny among the ranks, to nip his insolence in the bud, Peter had to be punished.

Would I have been less affronted had he not been obvious? "No one has treated me this poorly before, not professionally or otherwise," Peter ascertained. And, just as he expected, sadly, no one came to his defence, not even Stein. With certainty he knew this to be a neatly sewn up fiefdom. The chairman kept a very tight rein on the entire organisation.

They served a feast for lunch. At the table, the people who had spent the morning feeling ill at ease now ate with affected gusto. His appetite having deserted him, regrettably Peter could only toy with his food. Dejected, he worked to repel encroaching cynicism by remembering what his parents said about it: "Cynicism is not particularly conducive to retaining wonder." There was too much of it, as it happened. It was everywhere one looked nowadays. His parents did not encourage it in their children. Anyone could sit back and take the cynical view, but what good would come of it?

"The thing now is to keep myself from falling prey and getting stuck in a rut. It is far too easy to be cynical," Peter determined, "to merely sit on the sidelines and fling accusations about." It was his opinion that taking that road was a cop-out. Where was the challenge? It lacked imagination, and to encourage it was criminal.

At this table too, the chairman dominated the conversation. The topic of choice was now his house on Bygdøy, an island in the Oslo fjord where Norway's monarch, King Harald, had one of his residences. Apparently, the value of Nesheim's property had gone through the roof. With undisguised delight, he gave them the exact value of a square metre, eliciting nods and smiles of polite approval around the table.

"And this was supposedly a working luncheon," Peter thought.

For the afternoon session, set aside to review the foundation's finances, though the chairman took his rightful seat at the head of the table, he was to all intents and purposes absent, as he slept off his lunch. Respecting his ripe old age and veteran status, his colleagues permitted him his nap and spoke in soft tones. Needless to say, the accounts were approved in his absence.

"What a lesson!" Peter thought as confirmation of the kind of man the chairman was firmly crystallized in mind. He was one to enjoy any privilege conferred upon him without making good on the corresponding trust and responsibility that came with it. Here was man who adored his own voice and had no problem failing to provide vital checks and balances the foundation needed to thrive. This attitude was no doubt, shared by all the board members. He had heard no dissent. Paid handsomely for a fairly prestigious public service position, why did they simply not do their jobs?

With disbelief he recalled the two female board members sitting quietly and merely looking on as the chairman dismissed Elise as an irrational woman.

If a lesson on disillusionment had ever been planned, Peter did not think it would have been better than the one he had witnessed today. He thought of the qualities one gained with age and wisdom came first to mind. Along life's journey, it was expected that one would come by some wisdom. Age many believed, bestowed wisdom on people. It was one of the perks of a long life. To have lived as long as Mr Nesheim, and not to have acquired any wisdom, ought to be worrying.

He had treated Peter with contempt, inviting him to speak and suddenly withdrawing the privilege. Everyone deserved to be treated with respect and dignity. But how does one bestow dignity on a rude, old man? One with a misconstrued sense of self-worth and entitlement, which encouraged him to bully those he was supposed to lead, nurture and inspire. To think, Nesheim was a board member for another five organizations!

"Are there no others deserving of the honour? And, in the end, to whose benefit?" he desired to know. It was precisely this behaviour that held them back. Who could forget that it was Mr Nesheim's generation who sat on information about the detrimental effects of oil on the environment for four decades? This generation's lack of urgency in matters pertaining to the environment had astounded him before, and now it was clear that this very attitude held them back still. If there were people out there who had placed their trust in such organisations solving the dire problems faced by Earth and its inhabitants, sadly, he would have to tell them to think again.

Peter was glad he had been afforded the opportunity to see the board in action. This experience, jarring as it was, had at least answered a lot of questions that had been plaguing him. "This lot did not care about anyone or anything but themselves. Perhaps, this is what Maiken had seemed on the cusp of telling him."

Then he remembered something he had overheard at the office – no one working at North Marine Foundation remembered the accounts ever being audited. Even though only four hours away by train, no one in the capital saw the need to check on them either. They were apparently more than satisfied with the annual reports sent to them. Reports, he now knew were written by external consultants. Lacking the competence or professional pride to write their own annual progress report, the foundation commissioned a consultant to do it for them. And yet one of the comparative advantages the organization flaunted far and wide, Peter noted, was its capacity building expertise. They had earmarked resources and a whole department to helping other organisations operate more efficiently and effectively. Peter felt like crying at the irony.

On the way to the train station, he checked his phone for messages. Alex had sent him an email:

Hi Peter, my award ceremony is next week. Ask your boss for permission to attend. Will call later with the details. Can't wait to see you!

Love, Alex

PART III

16. *Vail*

At noon, on Friday, during the second week of December, Marjorie Keegan called to her husband upstairs to come down. Coming promptly into sight on the landing, she watched with a smile on her face as he walked down the stairs − a smile of gums only, thus appearing to her husband as though she had lost her teeth.

A frown creased his forehead, "can't she wait to get rid of me?" he wondered warily, once again unsettled by the undecipherable smile. Often in the past, he had asked her not to smile at him in this manner, but his pleas had fallen on deaf ears.

When he reached her, she firmly placed her possessive arms around his neck. Freeing him from her embrace, she saw the need to set right his blazer, straighten the collar of his shirt, and neatly draped a colourful scarf around his neck. Picking up his briefcase and coat, she asked with a smile to melt any heart if he was ready.

He kissed her lips gently, "yes, but I do wish you were coming."

Though she raised her brows in resignation, Marjorie did not speak. Enough had been said on the matter. They walked to the car in silence and while Joe put his suitcase in the trunk, she placed his hand luggage on the backseat, closed the door and installed herself in the driver's seat. Driving her husband to the airport was her way of making amends for not accompanying him.

Looking at his wife drive, Joe admitted his preference for her driving him. His rational mind immediately reminded him, however, that this was beside the point. Mr Kruger, the driver, and not his wife, should be driving him. Marjorie was stubborn though and insisted on driving. Careful of blurring the boundary between the servants and himself, he had not driven in years.

Leaving their neighbourhood of Beaver Brook in Vail, Colorado, they drove through the small town of Avon and several miles later, turned onto Interstate 70 in the direction of Gypsum and Eagle County Airport.

Regarding her husband sitting quietly beside her, Marjorie determined that his mind had already departed. Unperturbed, her thoughts turned to their children, her face suddenly growing pert as she cast her mind back to their toddler years. To faces mostly jolly, except when their cheeks turned ruby and warned her of coming molars. To their diaper-clad bottoms toddling around the house, swaying from side to side much like Donald Duck's would. To chubby legs with a fold at mid-thigh, which had run much faster than she had thought them capable. Their interaction with their surroundings and toys had captivated her. Theirs had been a curiosity that could not have been bettered.

Surprisingly, in spite of this curiosity, they had also possessed a wondrous sort of patience when engaged in a task, the exquisite kind required to fill a teacup with water using a teaspoon. Observing them, Marjorie had concluded that repetition was indeed the way to perfection. On matters less pleasant now, she remembered the fever and crying those molars brought along in the few days before they surfaced.

Fortunately for her, with the help of the housekeeper, Maria, raising the children did not get out of hand. Hardly rushed off her feet, she had had the time to enjoy them. Suddenly nostalgic, "did I prefer them when they were younger?" she deliberated. She quickly dismissed the thought; had she not learned that every moment in life was to be cherished? Recently, she had been impressing on herself, the importance of living in the moment. While engaging fully with the children on the way to school, she returned to savour her morning coffee in a quiet house and later in the day happily dined amid her children's boisterous conversations. With this realisation she could not comprehend why nostalgia had plagued her these past few weeks.

Lately, chauffeuring them from one place to the next seemed to require most of Marjorie's time. Wistfully, she recalled serene mornings when her young children had woken up naturally, on their own volition. There had been plenty of time then. In those days, the only events pencilled in on their schedule were the naps. To start with, there had been a midmorning nap for the baby of the moment and later, one for everybody. What she had come to dub 'morning madness' was something unknown at the time. The mad rush in order to be punctual for school came later. Despite her careful planning, their pace was all too often still rather frantic, what with the social events and the sports activities! Truly, if she did not take the time to drive them, then she would barely see her children.

"Marjorie, I am glad you're driving me, honey," Joe said, briefly patting her knee.

"You're welcome."

The pair smiled at one another and returned to their preoccupations.

Though intent on keeping her eyes on the road, when her glance strayed to the forest on the mountain slopes, she observed with sadness that, where there had once been forests of green, there was now starkly contrasting patches of brown and green. "What a shame it is that the trees in Colorado are dying. What will the mountains be without the trees?" she wondered, the thought of them bared to the elements causing her unease. "No, it will not be the same without the forest."

Enthralled at first glance by the mountains, the decision to make a home in this delightful habitat was the easiest one she had ever made. And Marjorie's first trip to Colorado was without question the best journey she had ever taken. She had travelled widely since, and in better style and comfort, but for its sheer sense of adventure, that cross-country road trip was still firmly at the top of her list. She and her childhood friends, Marcy and Jessica, had spent a good month planning it, painstakingly plotting the route and accommodation options with the aid of the latest Triple A maps and travel guides.

However, just before they left, they discovered that their plans were much too restrictive and had abandoned them.

"Where is our sense of adventure?" they had asked each other.

Challenging their stringent plans, they let them fall by the wayside in favour of a single guiding rule for the trip: that they arrived at their destination the day before they were to report for work. That principle and a week of traveling time was all their travel plans finally amounted to. Armed thus with a sense of adventure and the possibility to make spur-of-the-moment decisions and take the road less travelled, they had left Fairfax County in Virginia, crossed the Potomac River just north of Washington DC, and then veered westwards.

On state highways and meandering local roads they drove through the picturesque towns of Maryland and Pennsylvania. Upon reaching the Appalachians, along the way, they stopped to admire the view, take pictures, fill up on gas and sample the food offerings. By the time darkness fell, they had found a place to spend the night. With some regret they descended the magnificent mountain range and spent the day in St Louis, at the Gateway Arch, designed by the famous Finnish American architect, Eero Saarinen, and spent hours exploring the Lewis and Clark Museum.

Memorable was the lift to take them up the Archway. It had travelled sideways and up much like a funicular. And the space inside, how cramped it had been! Packed in tightly, there was not an inch to spare: "How easy it must be to get on each other's nerves in here," Marjorie had thought. Once they reached the top, she had gladly stepped out of confinement to stand at one of the few small windows availing her of the city's spread. Her eyes had roamed the sprawling skyline with interest. On display were man's ingenuity and his efforts to tame his environment. Intimidated by the city's size, she had drawn comfort from her friends beside her and had proceeded to soak it all in. She had crossed over to a window on the other side to look into the distance towards Illinois. But when she had looked down, she had gazed at the Mississippi River. The water was smooth, its colour a muddy brown, but of utmost importance to Marjorie was *the fact that the river flowed at all.*

Once more, as was the case when she looked at rivers, her hang-up about them stirred up twinges in her tummy. "All streams flow into the sea and yet the sea is never full," she had impulsively recited. This preoccupation of hers about rivers being able to flow smoothly and unimpeded to the sea was now a fixture in her life. The Bible verse that was meant to be reassuring when Father Boyd read it to the congregation, all those years ago, actually had the opposite effect on her. Her tender mind had envisioned the seas and oceans of the world filled to the brim and the rivers stagnant, with nowhere to flow, but right back to the muddy fields and meadows from which they hailed. And some of that water had found its way to her doorstep. Terrified, she still carried that vision around. Yes, it was uncanny, but the vision had stuck in her mind. What if the sea filled up? What would happen then?

Her mother often tried to reassure her by saying: "Honey, children your age have a wild imagination." But this reassurance had offered her no consolation. Perhaps her mother's words would have been comforting had she not experienced floods first-hand.

Beholding the indomitable Mississippi from the Archway had reminded her that the gullies and the brooks which flowed into streams and rivers would in turn find their way to her. Her journey through the Great Plains was to be long and her responsibilities would become greater with each mile before she finally drained out to sea. "The plains owe her a debt of gratitude, since they rely on her to drain them. But what an adventure," and at the thought, the idea of a future trip South took form. Taking a measured look at her friends standing beside her once again, she had searched for a way to persuade them to join her. "It will not be difficult," she had slyly resolved when she had found the perfect argument.

Inevitably, at her elevation, a sense of freedom and invincibility had pervaded her. And, she had been convinced, her own adventure had yet to begin. It was this sense that sustained her on the endless, straight highways of Kansas, surrounded by the rolling prairies from where she could see for miles and miles ahead, but only, more of the same terrain.

Seeking out points of interest from the tedious landscape, she had spotted trees that appeared to nestle in very small numbers to the bosoms of streams. "An oasis," she had thought, curious about the type of animals that sought refuge there. Grinning, she had surmised that the creatures in question had to be those accustomed to sharing space with cows, which there was an abundance of in Kansas.

When her turn to drive came along, it conferred the privilege to pick the music. She had chosen something they could all sing along to, something popular at the time; something to keep her eyes trained on the road, but long forgotten since. Crossing into the great State of Colorado, her curiosity could barely be contained, and she had sat up straighter in her seat. But it was not until a couple of hours later that she was fully rewarded. Suddenly at a distance, as if they just sprouted out of the ground, stood the majestic Rocky Mountains; rock-strewn and brown, their given name suiting them down to the ground.

Then Joe cut into her thoughts, by saying, "here we are. By the way, did I mention I am going to Canada on Sunday?"

"Yes, darling, you did," she answered, as the excitement from her memories kindled her smile.

Noticing her elation, Joe was baffled, "I'd rather not be accused of neglecting to mention it. Anyway, you have my schedule," he said looking rather bereft as he got out of the car.

Leaving him at the airport, she drove to pick up the children from school and, on the way she recalled that the trip to the South never did transpire. And as for her friends, she had not seen them in years. "I was just a girl then, so young." Looking into the rear-view mirror, at the elegant, grown up woman staring back at her, she couldn't help but wonder what ever became of that girl. The culprit, she grudgingly conceded, was time. "Time was to blame," she decried, for nudging her along and for chipping away at the girl and, finally, for transposing her with a woman. A woman she herself, on occasion, barely recognized. Had she seen it coming, she would have tried to cling on. Pushed so far along, however, clinging on then seemed ridiculous. Had her permission been sought, she might have borne it better. But all this, had been done to her on the sly. She had had no say in the matter.

Eventually, like all those who had come before, she too, got used to not being a girl. What sat very poorly with her still, however, was the fact that she was no longer her daddy's girl. "I cannot get over him," she remarked softly. "I cannot get over either of them; of losing them both."

Scrutinising her life, "what haven't I seen?" she asked. Married at twenty-four to a man fourteen years her senior, her nuptials came hand-in-hand with duties that demanded her constant attention. Early in her marriage, she had had two main occupations: entertaining and being entertained. She was either the consummate hostess for her husband or accompanying him to events for the sole purpose of consorting. The time they had spent thus engaged was shocking to her and it was not until after she had delivered their first child that she was able to beg off the socializing madness.

In a matter-of-fact way, she accepted that marriage had changed her. Those who vowed marriage would not change them in any fundamental way were surely naïve and misguided. Why marry at all if you weren't yearning to be transformed in wonderful ways by love and commitment? How could two separate households successfully merge without adaptation? And throughout the years, marriage had continued to mould, mature and inspire her.

Having said that, of all her experiences, the loss of her father and brother in a car accident had without question changed her the most. The pain broke her heart. Out of sheer self-preservation, in the third week after the funeral, her mind took her in hand and numbed her senses so that, in place of her essence, was a void. For months on end after that, she had inhabited a place where nothing could touch or harm her. Grief had isolated her splendidly. Even Joe's repeated acts of kindness went unheeded. As for something to give, she had had nothing. Nothing to give to baby Rosie, either!

The only thing that remained vivid in her barren mind and existence were the arrested expressions she recalled unremittingly on the faces of her lost loved ones; they had plagued her mercilessly since the day of the funeral. Leading up to the appointed funeral time, she and her mother had stood at the door of the funeral home waiting to be let in. Once inside, she had timidly walked behind her mom with her face tilted towards the carpeted floor, stopping on cue when her mother did.

"Come Marjorie. Say goodbye to Daddy and Tim," she had heard her say.

Sidestepping her to stand right beside the coffins, she finally got to see them. She had stared at two strangers who bore an odd, uncanny resemblance to her father and brother. Yes, the bodies of her father and brother lay before her, and yet their expressions were fallacious; they were not those of anyone she had known. They were simply unrecognisable; something was terribly, terribly wrong. Suddenly, at that moment, the fact that her father and Tim had ceased to be, struck her with brutal force. Their essence was clearly missing. Her heart had cringed violently at the poignant lack of life in her relatives.

Deep within her chest, her breath had suddenly halted, causing her considerable physical pain. "To catch one's breath and not to have it returned. What's that like?" her stunned mind had numbly asked, certain then, that it was in fact too late to bid them farewell. It was futile. And, worse still, she had fallen terribly short by not giving any thought to what she would see beforehand. How altogether unprepared she had been. She had established death a far cry from life and had observed how ugliness became death. There was no beauty to be found in death. Before the funeral she had been troubled by the thought of burying them. Having set eyes on them, the idea was no longer problematic. As for her, well, she was never to be the same.

Yes, she had met all kinds of people and could lay claim to all sorts of experiences, the sum of which was the woman she had become. At forty, Marjorie judged her maturity to have peaked. As such, she was confident that nothing in life would ever again jolt her.

Arriving at the school, the children hopped into the car and sank into their seats with sighs of relief. The week had taken its toll on them and the little chatter they could muster on the way home merely served a practical purpose.

"What's for dinner?" Niles wished to know.

"Roast chicken. Maria is making your favourite."

"Thanks Mom," he responded shyly.

Marjorie could tell her teenage son was famished. His consumption of food was astronomical. It was no wonder he shot up the way he did.

"Did you download the movie, Mom?" Lily eagerly asked.

"Which movie is that?" she answered, feigning ignorance.

"Mom!" Lily exclaimed.

She looked in her rear-view mirror at Rosie all the way in the back, in her own world listening to music on her headphones and noticed that Violet beside her had fallen asleep. Seeing Violet sleeping soundly reaffirmed her decree that, Friday evenings in the Keegan household were to be spent at home. By Friday, they were all in need of a restful evening.

At a half past three in the afternoon, Marjorie arrived at home and drove into the garage. The children, including Violet, who was woken up by the burst of chatter from her siblings, dashed from the car with their backpacks and ran up the few steps into the house. In the hallway they dropped their bags, threw off their shoes and scuttled to the bathroom to wash their hands. After that initial flurry of activity, a sudden quiet mercifully descended, the only sign of life in the house the clicking of cutlery from the dining room where Maria was setting the table. The children had disappeared to the comfort and solitude of their rooms upstairs.

Marjorie walked into the hallway to find her way blocked by bags and shoes strewn all over the floor. Placing her hands on her hips she looked at the mess with dismay, shaking her head. Resisting the urge to shout admonishments, she wondered plaintively if the kids had finally worn her down.

Joining Maria in the kitchen, she lent a hand to the dinner preparations and, at four o'clock sharp dinner was served. With the children weaned off their picky eating habits, the meal was a pleasant affair. Accustomed to their father's absence, the children did not so much as ask about his whereabouts. Marjorie, nonetheless, informed them that their father would be spending the weekend in Washington D.C.

At nine o'clock she tucked Lily and Violet snugly in their cosy beds and kissed them goodnight. Rosie and Niles no longer required putting to bed, but she went to bid them goodnight and encouraged them to go to sleep.

Having locked the house for the night, she took a long lazy bath. After her bath, she put on her comfy flannel pyjamas, something she wore without fail whenever her husband was not at home. She settled down to watch the news in bed and waited for his ritual phone call. When it finally came an hour later, she cheerfully asked about his trip, permitting him ample time to talk. Joe was always very talkative when checking in with her from afar. He recounted bits of gossip he had overheard from the crew of his jet when they had chatted with each other. Eddie, the young steward had just been jilted by his girlfriend and was crushed.

Marjorie smiled with satisfaction, "he won't be crying on Joe's shoulder. Men just aren't equipped to do that." The idea of a woman crying on her husband's shoulder did not sit well with her. Once she became Mrs Keegan, she had taken the necessary measures and Keegan One, her husband's jet, had been a man's domain for many years now. After saying goodnight to Joe, she fell asleep almost instantly.

17. The chief executive

At seven o'clock on a Saturday evening, a limousine pulled up at the All Seasons Hotel in Georgetown, Washington D.C. The driver from the corporate limousine service called the reception desk to inform them that a chauffeur was waiting for Mr Joseph Keegan. When the telephone rang, Joe stood before a mirror, attired in his formal evening dress, inspecting an outstandingly groomed, middle-aged man with a shrewd glint in his eye, the kind that defied anyone to cross him. A decided smugness about his mouth underpinned what his impeccable clothing said about him. The man hailed from the secure classes, from that group of people who were disengaged from the endless, exhausting battle of making ends meet, and lived not on their capital, but on the dividends earned by their many and varied investments.

Through the generations, his class had learned the very important lesson of not storing all of one's eggs in one basket, but, rather, cleverly scattered them about so that any unfortunate downturn in the markets was in time absorbed. Even better, some of these nest eggs were hidden in places that were unburdened by taxes. In this manner, their fortunes could be secured and cultivated, and their affluence perpetuated across the generations.

His glance did not linger, but quickly skimmed down to his broad shoulders, before it lowered to his lean waist and, finally, ran down his long but well-built, athletic legs. Pleased by his fitness, he demurely grinned at his image.

Arriving at the gleaming black limousine exactly five minutes after the call, the chauffeur opened the door for him. He was not the same driver who had spoken to the receptionist. Joe slipped into the luxuriously appointed backseat while paying no heed to the driver. If everything went according to plan, which it should, if they knew what was good for them, he left them alone. He, for one, took great pride in not fraternising with the help and had no understanding for people who pandered, rather pretentiously, it must be said, to their servants. It was his opinion that such people profoundly misunderstood the dynamics of such a relationship.

Joe sat happily at ease in the limousine preoccupied with the corporate event he was on his way to attend. This particular dinner party was one he could ill afford to miss; all the captains of industry would be there – the manufacturers, the traders and, not least, the bankers. On this evening, as so often in the past, the unifying characteristics of these high-flyers would be on full display: they would be relentlessly fishing for information, for any scrap of market intelligence, while masking ulterior aims, feigning surprise and pretending to be indifferent. What a circus! Joe had long ago accepted this behaviour as an unavoidable part of the cat-and-mouse game they all played, even he. But he had also become adept at allowing their sycophantic, disingenuous pronouncements to enter into one ear and escape in an instant through the other.

Though not immune, to feigning either surprise or disinterest, lately Joe could not shake the feeling he had begun to overplay his hand. Had he any caution in him, he would have investigated the reason he felt this way. But, having amassed more than his fair share of confidence over the years, he had thrown all caution to the wind. His indiscretion was deliberate; he now permitted himself to ignore his gut instincts in the belief that second-guessing himself was a sign of weakness. It could no longer do. And so, he had played on.

His enjoyment of the game was only stymied by his perceived lack of honour in those with whom he played, his counterparts. Usually such feelings surfaced when his hand was weak. Then, he would notice that his people had no scruples, and would find that he no longer knew what to make of them. Perceiving their excesses repugnant, he would wonder why he ever thought he fit in.

With regard to the investment bankers, such thoughts occurred frequently now. Their recent gambles had weakened his hand considerably, costing him a great deal of money. He was singularly focused on recouping these losses. Even though it was still floating, his boat, so to speak, had been thoroughly rocked. As far as he could tell, none of them had suffered similar losses. They had weathered the storm very well. Reeling with disappointment and aghast at their audacity, with severity he concluded: "They don't possess any integrity, not a shred!"

The stock exchange crash of 2008 had taken the shine off. The extent of the deceit revealed these past years had left him with a bleak outlook and a future that looked increasingly difficult to secure. More than ever, the times seemed precarious. Like many others, he too had tried to understand how it could have gone so wrong so quickly, catching almost everyone by surprise. The point that became clear to him was that the magicians on Wall Street had somehow believed they could make something out of nothing. And they had made a great success of keeping up appearances right up until that 'something' again inevitably became nothing. Why had his fund manager not seen the warning signs? He should have listened to that investment analyst when she warned about derivatives. Derivatives, he later learned were equities derived from thin air. Most brokers didn't even understand what they were trading, much less anything about the complex formulae devised to create them.

The mystery and very sore point for Joe was why his manager – and everyone else for that matter – had not looked into the expert's warning before dismissing her. Still on the subject, while wondering what had happened to their curiosity: "This is what they are there for, after all, and it's why people like me pay them generously. It is to avoid precisely these types of calamitous surprises."

To no avail, he tried to remember the woman's name. Being someone who trained his mind for the purpose of improving his mental faculties and in particular his memory Joe was convinced that he had forgotten by way of self-preservation. This clearly, was a matter of his mind protecting him from memories that would cause him further pain. Joe felt betrayed by everyone involved in the financial markets, the banks and their boards, the traders, investment fund managers and insurance companies, the financial regulators and rating agencies, politicians…everyone. What chance did the poor investor have in the face of what one would be forgiven for believing was naked collusion? The answer to this question reinforced his earlier determination that, somewhere along the way, it had all gone very wrong. Surely the Stock Exchange was not designed to function in this manner, whereby the bankers, insurance companies and the rating agencies all slept in the same bed? Where subprime investments received an undeserved triple A rating!

To get the clarity he needed, Joe had attended the congressional hearings and had seen with his own eyes the bosses from the rating agencies absolve themselves of any responsibility whatsoever, explaining to Congress that their role was to merely proffer 'opinions'. He had watched them essentially equate their professional opinion to that of any Tom, Dick or Sally, however well or ill - informed about the vagaries and complexities of financial markets. So, at the end of the day, their judgements should not be taken seriously. Joe had been stunned by the shameless spectacle of the rating agencies, and he had considered them finished: "No one will ever take them seriously after this!" And yet, how wrong he had been; nothing had changed. They were still peddling their worthless opinions and, dismayingly, no one batted an eye.

By all accounts, Joe longed to forget, but he knew that to be easier said than done. The stress of it all had caught up to him and clung to him like glue. A substantial portion of his fortune had evaporated that year. "Pompous idiots," he thought them then, still experiencing anger from the events. When the exact sum of his loss came to mind, he changed the adjective 'idiot' to something much harsher.

As far as he was concerned, the spell was broken and, from where he stood, the magic was long gone. He had not taken investment advice from anyone since. He could no longer believe a word they said to him. What free forces of the market were they talking about when behind the scenes they were preoccupied with fixing things to their advantage?

Though getting it right before all this madness was impossible without some degree of luck, competence and integrity had gone into the mix then. Yes, there had been that before but now, all that was left was fixing the game to one's own advantage. "You can't put anything past these people," he thought sardonically, "not with what we know now."

How could he place his faith in the system when it gave reign to the world's greatest fraudster? The enablers of the system had worshipped at his feet while he stole people's pensions right from under their noses. Shaking his head in despair, he wondered why it had taken so long for him to recognise that it was all one big farce. They may call him mad if they wished, but he reckoned his guess was as good as theirs' and he, for one, would no longer be throwing any of his good money their way.

"No," he admitted it to himself once again, the Annual Commerce Convention in Washington DC, no longer inspired joy. Then again, however mundane and chore-like it now felt to him, if he didn't play along and show up at these events, how else was he to know what those fellows were up to?

"I can play their racket just as well as they do, and, if I put my mind to it, perhaps even better," he thought.

Looking back, he could hardly believe he had at one time actually looked forward to this gathering. In the past, he and his wife had happily made a weekend getaway of the occasion. Arriving late on a Friday evening, usually they had splurged on room service. Worn by the busy week and the long flight from Vail, they took long baths and savoured each other's company, for once uninterrupted. All this had a wondrous effect on his wife and, in particular, her need for affection.

Abandoning all restraints, alone with her, he was able to shower her with the attention she deserved. No one would walk in on them there, not the children, and certainly not Rosie. With a smile, he remembered the instance Rosie nearly caught them out. On a Saturday morning, he awoke at six o'clock and discovering that he was at home with his wife lying beside him, there was nothing else for it, but to wake her up. His whispering to Marjorie enquiring if she was awake, of course, woke her. Of all the people he knew, she was the lightest sleeper. Bringing up four children, he supposed, would have that effect. As a fairly substantial part of mothering was listening out for the children, in time, her antennae picked up on absolutely everything. Sometimes he wondered why he paid for a security system for the house when Marjorie would suffice.

Realising he was drifting, he retraced his thoughts to Rosie, at the time, only seven years old, and to her unannounced, early morning visit to their room. After Marjorie had woken up, his talk became enticingly sweet and her response accommodated the ritual of a Saturday morning seduction. They had heard footsteps to the bathroom and the sound of a toilet flushing, the faucet had run and closed. And then, heading straight to their bedroom, they had heard the same little footsteps, abruptly followed by the door being flung wide open, revealing a little round face with eyes smitten by an unchecked curiosity. "Were you guys making a baby, cause I thought I heard something?" Rosie had asked.

An excited glint appeared in his eyes then, as he was reminded that his one and only weakness was his wife. It was the only weakness he allowed, his one and only genuine vice. Taken on strict terms, however, the desire he felt for his wife was no vice; it was only natural and how it should be. It was a mystery that he considered it somehow immoral.

Further reminiscing about his children had Joe smiling even more broadly. His son Niles was smart and had a sense of cunning that pleased him. The boy, clearly had what it took to succeed and would no doubt, do very well. Tall, with a strong frame, there was a decided physical presence to him. Nothing put a wider smile on Joe's face than the thought of Niles carrying on the family name, exceeding his achievements as well as those of his forefathers. Niles would further build on the solid family foundations, just as he had done. Continuity, what else could conjure up a stronger sense of satisfaction than continuity?

Joe adored his children, whose beauty he in no small measure could credit his wife. Daughters Rosie, Lily and Violet were both attractive and charming. Some would equate charm with weakness, but not Joe. To wit, his wife was both charming *and* of strong character. He recalled the send-off she had treated him to the day before, and blushed. Lingering, evocative memory of their latest liaison soon meant he was compelled to readjust his position in the back of the limo. Joe glanced self-consciously at the driver, but the man's eyes remained fixed on the road ahead.

Alarmed by his reaction, he worked on steadying himself by reverting to a safer theme, his business. "If the children wish to join the family business," he thought smugly, "then there is room for all of them. If my daughters are so inclined, they will have no trouble finding suitors." That his daughters might wish to do both did not even occur to Joe. Unfair though it might be, as good-looking as they were, he knew life would be kind to his girls. He wished that was not the case, for he favoured merit over physical attributes, fully aware this opinion betrayed the executive in him. For when it came time to choose a wife, it was beauty he was taken by, not discernment or intelligence.

To him, these fine qualities, which his wife possessed in abundance, were merely a bonus. During his courtship, he had not sought them out. It was in the course of their marriage that these qualities rather quickly became apparent and it seemed to Joe at the time that their value would only appreciate over the years. With the birth of his children came the realisation that having his progeny raised by a daft woman would have been a grave mistake. With his children's upbringing at stake, the value of his wife's qualities had, in his eyes, soared.

On the morning of the convention, with a skip in her step, Marjorie would plant a kiss on his forehead, glide out of the room, and take the elevator down to the hotel spa. Choice treatments would be lavished on her by the attentive spa staff, as a part of her preparations for the

Composed as could be, his piercing gaze fixed on Joe, "good evening Mr Keegan. I'm afraid your plans for the evening have just changed."

18.   Chesapeake Bay

When Joe Keegan came to, he was lying flat in bed. His head rested on a firm comfortable pillow. Sighing contentedly, he turned onto his side and pulled the bedding around his neck. He experienced a gentle rocking, which he recognised instantly. "I'm on a boat?" he queried in alarm. During his deep slumber, the events of the previous evening had been expunged from his mind and he had slept the sleep of a free man. With a start, vivid memory of the incident in the car returned.

Without warning, his breathing accelerated, as did his heartbeat, whose intense pounding he now felt in his chest cavity. His mouth ran dry. As the energy required for the impending escapade was released into his blood stream, he trembled from head to toe while his body wound itself into a coil, ready to unwind into a life-saving sprint at a moment's notice. All this was achieved instinctively, his body seemingly having acquired a mind of its own.

He quickly raised his head. This motion tugged uncomfortably at his dazed head and the bright light pouring in from the portholes to which his eyes were drawn, made him blink furiously. His recoil from the blinding light had the effect of casting his glance on the immaculate wooden panelling of the cabin walls. Captivated, his eyes traced the panelling upwards to an elegant white ceiling with recessed lighting, pausing for a moment before resting on the outstanding cabinetry on the wall opposite the bed he lay on. A well-padded leather armchair on his side of the bed came finally into view.

The splendour of the cabin took Joe's breath away. He propped himself up and peered uneasily around. "Whoever they are, they have excellent taste," he said softly, no longer in doubt he was on a luxury yacht, wondering then if he somehow ought to be reassured by that fact. The answer was a resounding, "no." These people were kidnappers!

Since he was a cornered creature, he understood that all the energy coursing through him would be for nought. Curious about how long he had been held captive, he quickly lifted up his wrist to look at his watch and, with a mixture of awe and disappointment, saw that it was only nine in the morning. Being a Sunday, merely a few hours after the corporate event, it was surely too early for anyone to have missed him. In a state of agitation, his thumb frantically rubbed the face of his watch. All at once it struck him as very odd that his expensive timepiece was still in his possession. Peering at it as he lifted his hand up high made him aware that his wrists were free, as were his ankles.

Astonished, Joe rose quickly to stand on tottering legs; he recognised his need for support and leaned against the wall. Standing there unsteadily, the thought occurred to him that he ought to have a plan. "But what sort of plan?" he mumbled feebly. As his trembling eased, he finally grasped that he was in a state of physical shock. Curiosity got the better of him; he cautiously made his way to the door to see if it could be unlocked. With a turn on the handle, remarkably it swung wide open, leaving him face to face with his two captors. He recognised one of them as the young man from the night before. Both men were on their feet and paid him their undivided attention.

"They are very young, can't be more than twenty-five," he judged, immediately struck by their resemblance to Oliver, his public relations director, who remained blissfully unaware that his employment at Keegan Oil was influenced by an article Joe had read in one of his business journals. While making perfect sense, the article had nonetheless surprised Joe.

Human beings possess an inborn instinct to nurture their young. A baby's soft round features and its helplessness were designed to captivate its parent's attention to this very end.

Joe was acquainted with these facts and had been impatient for the author to get to the point.

This instinct is so deeply ingrained in people that, subconsciously, they extended the courtesy to grown-ups still in possession of facial features associated with babies.

Slightly appalled the thought had not, before crossed his mind, he had been compelled to test the theory.

Oliver's face lacked chiselled features and firmness. It seemed to have prematurely stopped forming. His small forehead sloped down towards moist brown eyes, a button nose and a small mouth to join up with a soft chin, resulting in a nicely rounded face, a countenance that inspired cooing. Oliver's performance went well beyond Joe's expectations, leading him to believe that the article had indeed been right. On many an occasion, Joe had watched Oliver explain away murder on behalf of Keegan Oil to a bunch of cooing reporters.

Studying his captors very closely, he noted their lack of prominent features. They neither had high cheekbones nor strong jawlines. Everything about their faces was nice and rounded too. At a loss to understand why their looks were suddenly a source of annoyance, Joe was irritated. Why should he give a toss about their looks? But then he noticed that, unlike Oliver, their pudginess was limited to their faces. Beneath their clothes, he could clearly make out strong, athletic and trim outlines. There was no sign of softness there. Joe was awestruck.

The young men shared similar builds, except for the few inches the young man from the night before had over his companion. He detected an affinity between them so strong that Joe was convinced they were siblings. With arrogance, he pronounced them pathetic human specimens. His choice of the word specimen was calculated; to despise them fully he had to perceive them as odd human beings.

The one from the night before now addressed him, "good morning, Mr Keegan. Would you care for a cup of coffee?"

Joe was motionless, unable to respond. His initial assessment of the pair, intended to give him a psychological edge over them, was not as effective as he had hoped. The sight of them with their baby faces standing formidably still, without so much as a twitch, made him lose his nerve. How men with their faces pulled off such formidable stances was incomprehensible to him. He was certain, at the same time that the formidability was not imagined. Its daunting and impressive effect was as authentic as it was unnerving. He felt inadequate, in fact hopelessly unprepared, and couldn't help but notice that his own sudden entry seemed to have had no effect on them whatsoever. They contemplated him with a serene, enviable calm. And now that he spoke, the young man betrayed his English roots. Why had he not noticed that the night before? Deliberating their motives, he wondered with a growing sense of fear, what it was they were after exactly. And now they asked him to play guest!

While the other young man fetched coffee, the one who spoke to him earlier motioned, "please have a seat," pointing to a part of the sectional sofa in the dining area of the yacht. Still weak at the knees, Joe took a few steps forward and sat down gratefully. When the hot cup of coffee was placed in his hands, he habitually lifted it to his mouth and drank from it. It was coffee the way he liked it.

The bearer of the coffee, the shorter of the two, sat down facing him, while the other, remained standing a few feet away with a clear view of their captive.

"Mr Keegan," the one seated said looking him in the eye, "lend me your ears for a moment, please." This one was obviously English too.

Joe wished to answer with sarcasm, "I'm all ears." However, the earnestness with which the young man regarded and spoke to him stopped him in his tracks. Instead he found himself nodding robotically, silently, as he looked into the most remarkable pair of eyes he had ever beheld. Their other - worldly silver colouring and the unnaturally large and dark pupils entranced him.

"Did you know that, for untold years, astronomers and scientists have been scouring the universe, in fact, several different universes, in search of a planet like Earth? In 2006, amid considerable excitement, they reported that they had finally discovered one. It was similar, but not identical to Earth, with a surface temperature of 2,000 degrees Celsius. The primary cause for the excitement was the revelation that the distance between this planet and its sun is approximate to the distance between Earth and our sun. As I said earlier, they are similar but not the same, and not quite habitable either. And do you know how far away this remarkable planet is?"

He paused for the answer. More silence. "It is 25,000 light years away. Have you any idea how far away that is, Mr Keegan?"

Joe only shook his head.

"Of course, in the meantime, other planets have been found that have also aroused great scientific interest and caused much excitement. But none of them are Earth!"

Being trapped in the young man's gaze was paralysing. But Joe still recognised the passion in his eyes. Before now, he had even admired it in others. It was passion that compelled people to behave in extraordinary ways. Without passion, all there was left was mediocrity. Nothing of consequence was ever accomplished without it. Long ago, he himself had had this sort of passion and he had used it to build himself an empire. After inheriting what his father had started, he expanded the company beyond recognition. This young man was passionate and full of magnetism, but what was his purpose and where would this encounter lead?

"Are you a seafaring man, Mr Keegan? Have you heard of the Mariana Trench? It is the deepest trench in all of the oceans, with a floor 10,994 metres below the sea level. The creatures there live in complete darkness, the trench being too deep for the sun to penetrate. Nothing can grow at that depth and, as such, food for the creatures that live there floats down to them from above. At such a depth one would have expected the Mariana Trench to be utterly pristine, untouched by human influence. Some scientists had initially believed this to be the case, but do you know what they actually found when they sent an unmanned lander to the bottom to collect samples of life? Amongst others, they discovered crustaceans with bodies full of polychlorinated biphenyls and poly brominated diphenyl ethers. Now, of what use, to a little shrimp at the bottom of the ocean, is a body filled with fire retardant? Do you not see the role you are playing here? Nothing on Earth is pristine…not anymore. You are poisoning living organisms everywhere and, more so, human beings. You cannot even begin to imagine the consequences. And that's not to mention the effect all this has on our heredity."

Unnerved, Joe Keegan merely stared.

Eyeing him searchingly now, "Mr Keegan, we will no longer sit idly by while you and your sordid friends run amok and ravage the only planet and home we will ever have."

And Joe saw his eyes light up then, with emotion he could not place. Second-guessing himself he thought: "Revulsion perhaps, impatience and anger? An impassioned anger," though very uncertain about what he observed.

But when the young man next spoke, all emotion had disappeared from his eyes. "In case you were wondering, the velocity of light is 300,000 kilometres per second."

He allowed Joe time to let it sink in, before proceeding. "Now we find ourselves in an impossible situation, you are unrelenting. Your excesses and greed know no bounds. For profit, you will plunder, pollute and destroy. Are you aware that the amount of carbon dioxide in the atmosphere has reached unprecedented and unsustainable levels? Do you know that the lifespan of a carbon dioxide molecule is a thousand years? The fact that you are ruining everything for the rest of us does not even occur to you, does it? You are smug and dismissive of everyone who is not like you. You are blind to the needs and interests of every living being and to the planet itself, to everything except your own selfish ambition. How is it acceptable or satisfying in any way to terrorise people whose only misfortune is to live on lands, which contain something you desire for economic gain? Your search for new territory to plunder and devour, before you eagerly move on to the next 'big opportunity' is unrelenting. How much money does a person actually need for a happy and content lifetime on Earth? You behave as though your life is worth more than everybody else's simply because you are rich."

The young man stopped and observed Joe fixedly. Joe didn't comprehend why he had not cottoned on immediately. Was he thrown off by the setting? But now he understood; how well he understood. And the fear he felt before seemed now to have been no fear at all. "Who are these people?" he wondered.

"Here's how we'll proceed," he heard the young man continue. "You are to call your publicist and instruct her to arrange a press conference for ten o'clock tomorrow at your hotel. At this conference you will inform the press that you are moving to Alberta, Canada, to take up residence on the Potowak Indian reservation located downriver from the oil sands. This community's land is poisoned and the people there suffer acutely from all kinds of cancer. We're going to give you the chance to put your money where your mouth is, Mr Keegan. That shouldn't pose any problems, should it? After all, you appeared on television proclaiming that there were no toxins escaping from the wastewater reservoirs your company built upstream from the reservation. The trees you transplanted and the bison you relocated there are not convincing evidence of a toxin-free environment, not for us any way. We need something much more concrete than that and that will be you, Sir. You will be the King's guest and he, and the whole community are expecting you. You will hunt, fish and eat with him and his family. You are to be respectful and courteous at all times."

His face contorting in anger, Joe shouted, "who the hell do you think you are?" as the pride and defiant spirit that lived in Joe Keegan resurfaced. "You're holding me here against my will. You have kidnapped me; you've broken the law!"

"Do you really want to talk about the law? About matters pertaining to justice and equity, Mr Keegan? About integrity, principle and right-mindedness even? How about the principle that human life should be held in the highest esteem? As far as we can tell, by your actions you believe that the denigration, disenfranchisement and slaughter of people in the name of profit is not just legal, but perfectly above-board."

Joe wondered how one so young could have mastered such restraint and composure. "Who *are* these people?" he asked himself again. How wrong he had been to consider them unremarkable.

His interrogator saw that Joe would remain unresponsive. "Now that that's settled, we'll take you back to the hotel," he finished.

Joe's expression changed instantly; he stared at him in disbelief. What did he mean? Would they let him go just like that? Why did they go to all this trouble? His inability to comprehend the situation was losing him his grip. Unable to reconcile what he had heard, in confusion and rage he yelled: "How will you make me?"

The man standing came forward with a laptop and placed it on the table in front of Joe. Several minutes later when Joe looked up in horror the young man said: "You see, Mr Keegan, we don't have to make you; you will make yourself. You are on our radar around the clock now. In fact, we have been tracking you the last six hours. We will set your coordinates to the reservation as soon as you arrive. If you exit the boundaries of the reservation, which as I said will be precisely plotted, the implant will instantly kill you. But you will be the one to make that choice, not us. Likewise, if you attempt to remove the implant; the tag, that will kill you too."

His voice quavering, Joe articulated what had been on his mind from the moment he set eyes on the young men. "Who *are* you?"

In unison they replied: "Join us up on the deck and we'll show you."

"Did they practice that?" Joe wondered marvelling at the cohesive delivery of the sentence.

He followed one of them up to the deck, while the other followed in his wake. On the deck, Joe noticed that the yacht they were on was a Nautor's Swan, a high-performance, ocean-going, luxury sailing yacht. The Swan 120 Heritage no less! He had not seen this particular model up close before – it was simply magnificent! He might have known when he was inside the cabin. No one captured simplicity and elegance in boat design quite like the Finns. Theirs was the better boat, theirs was the real yacht, not his. And he could not lay claim to ever being in full sail; he had in fact never learned to sail. Yes, he had been at full throttle, but that was hardly the same thing.

Out there on the deck with the mast towering high above him, a wind blowing in his face, and the mild morning sun barely warming his back, he took a deep breath and wished he had been on that fantastic ocean-going boat under different circumstances. Much different circumstances indeed. He wished, too, that he had taken the time to master sailing. Looking at the men now, he could easily imagine them competent sailors. And in mind, he envisioned them setting sail. Both were light on their feet, their bodies tall and lithe, as they competently guided the yacht further out to the open sea. He looked up at the sails now bloated with wind, heard the water beneath whisper as it fell away from the hull. Other than that, the only sound to be heard was from the wind as it sent them on their way.

"Yes," he thought, reacquainting himself with the present, "they say the future will be all about the so-called clean energy powered by the wind and the sun. Even that old oilman from Texas had jumped onto that bandwagon. And a real boon he will be to the industry," he thought reflexively. Then again, hadn't the oilman merely embraced innovation? And wasn't he himself known for doing the same, for breaking the mould and pushing boundaries? Had he not also welcomed innovation with open arms?

Why a man with his money never took the time to properly enjoy life's delights seemed to him now the height of foolishness. And for a moment, he was at a loss as to understand why. "During the summers, I could have worked from my yacht and the family could have joined me. Everyone would have been happy." This hindsight stung even as it dawned on him that what truly made him happy was the thrill of the chase, the chase of the dollar at any cost.

Sensing apprehension from his captors, he paid closer attention. They took a quick glance at each other before taking off their shirts. From where he stood, Joe saw more of their fronts than backs, enough to confirm, however, that he had been right about their physiques. Instinctively, Joe thought it wise to remain a casual observer, a mere bystander, to the proceedings before him. The casual look he cast their way, therefore, only revealed musculature of excellent tone and strength. He perceived no intrigue or mystery.

While Joe sensed nothing out of the ordinary, someone with an inquisitive and educated eye would have gotten the subtlest of inklings that there was a good deal more to those beautiful bodies than met the eye. What would have become of this inclination had he had it, would have been interesting to observe. Having never encountered it before, would the interest have lasted long enough, to permit him opportunity to notice that something was amiss or would it simply have evaporated, being that in mind, there was no memory of this sort of thing?

The young men shed their garb to reveal swimming trunks. Whatever it was they meant to share with him, the seemingly ritual undressing was in no way incidental. "This is all part of their plan." Once more he observed the exchange of furtive glances. Joe was now quite sure that they were apprehensive, so he watched very closely as they slowly jutted out their chests in his direction. At that moment, horizontally arrayed operculum opened ever so slightly to reveal pulsating, red gills. Each chest revealed a set of six very thin, barely detectable orifices, with three slits on either side of their upper sternum, just beneath their collarbones.

Unable to control himself, Joe cried out in disbelief: "Good God, you are *fish!*" The alarm in his voice still reverberating, he wobbled from side to side. As Joe passed out, his legs buckled, and he hit the deck with a loud thud. The young men exchanged glances in amazement, giggled and then burst out laughing, long and hard, before crumpling to the deck.

"It certainly didn't take much to impress him," Peter remarked when they had finally calmed down. "At least he saved me from diving into the Chesapeake Bay." When they were past joking, both felt sad. If people reacted to them this way, it was best that their secret be kept and wondered if it had been wise to reveal their secret to Mr Keegan. Peter looked at his brother and articulated what was on both their minds, "mum and dad would not approve."

19.   Ichthys

"I am no longer my own man," Joe resolved on waking up slumped in the back seat beside one of his captors. A wave of grogginess stronger than he had experienced earlier that morning swamped his head and he was certain he had been drugged once more. "At least I'm not driving." Intended to encourage, the sentiment left Joe feeling rather pathetic instead. After years of being chauffeured around, of a pampered lifestyle, truth be told, the thought of getting behind the wheel now actually filled him with dread. "Where's the freedom in *that*?" he wondered dispiritedly.

They drove on a motorway chock-full of cars, in all likelihood, within the proximity of the city. As promised, he supposed that he was being taken back to the hotel. If ever there was a promise lacking in gratification, Joe felt that this was it. Avoiding eye contact with his young kidnapper seated beside him, he looked out the window divested of all interest in his surroundings, until he all of a sudden noticed from the corner of his eye a shinning silver fish emblem on the back of the car driving in the next lane. The glint of the sun had no doubt caught his eye. Curiosity prompted him to push his head forward for a clearer view of the passengers, but as it was a van, the limited sight made observation difficult and he wasn't quite sure what to make of the occupants.

Their eyes trained steadfastly on the road ahead, Joe's abductors betrayed no discernible interest in the van, which had not yet overtaken them. His own interest, therefore, began to seem somewhat absurd. But having for so long been surrounded by people who easily feigned emotion, his suspicion made it impossible to write off the van. He watched the vehicle for a while longer and then wondered if it indeed was trailing them. Was he simply being paranoid? Was his suspicion misplaced? Though he felt ridiculous, his watchful eyes continued to rove, searching the teeming traffic for the fish symbol.

"How many of them are there?" he wondered and seconds later mouthed to the window; "the fish people I mean," by way of clarifying his thoughts. In the past, when he had seen such an emblem, he had not spared it a second thought. Remembering these sightings as best as he could, he realised he had seen many cars with this particular emblem. Christians marked their cars with it. Niggling at his mind now was the question, "can I be certain of that knowing what I now know? Having seen, what I have seen with my own eyes?"

Aghast at the implication, Joe felt he really ought to just stop thinking, to turn off his irritatingly inquisitive mind. His thoughts flitted to the story of the early Christians who had adopted the fish as their secret emblem in times of great persecution. Determined to survive, they had developed an ingenious means of identifying other believers, of knowing whom they could trust. One simply drew an arch on the ground, half of the ichthys, the Greek word for fish - which in turn prompted the other party to complete it. "Very shrewd," he concluded in admiration.

Now that he was quite unexpectedly alert to it, the silver fish was all around. "Strange how things pop up everywhere when you take the least bit of interest," he thought vexed. Suddenly a symbol unlike the others, nonetheless a fish, but a fish with feet, caught his attention. The fish had four feet and the name Darwin was written in its confines. And he got the point: this was the fish with the famed feet to walk out of the sea. The fish species that took the leap from sea to land. Had he not been in his predicament, he would have laughed.

No longer his own master, it stood to reason, that his humour should now fail him miserably. "The evolutionists are blissfully unaware of the trend that is now headed in the opposite direction," he sardonically thought. And he would defy anyone to say they saw this coming. "Let them stand by their beliefs, it is their prerogative to do so," he expressed to himself with impish glee. Realizing it would be wrong of him to mock them, he relented but, not before pitying their circumstances. Surprisingly, his newly acquired knowledge pleased him. He was in on something; he had a secret. But where did all this leave the evolutionists? Thinking about his own pressing situation, he decided not to give the evolutionists any more thought.

For want of an uplifting preoccupation, Joe searched for an appropriate insignia for his fish people. Recognising their long torsos as evocative of swimmers, he was reminded of the great athlete from Philadelphia who had won Olympic gold medals by the handful. His body was like theirs, for he too had practically lived in the water. Sketching in his mind, Joe widened the chest to reveal gills, emulating those he had seen earlier, but more discernible, obvious even, and then placed the arms over the head, rather how he imagined a cliff diver would pose. He made sure it did not lack for modesty, before reducing it to miniature and casting it in silver. Pleased with his creation, Joe declared the figurine a fitting representation of those fortunate, or unfortunate enough, to be regressing to the sea.

Feeling particularly distressed, "where does all this leave me, now that my fate lies in the hands of others?" But he couldn't tell, he just didn't know anymore. Bewildered, he paused to question what he had seen. Could what I saw, be real? And as his mind went over the scene on the deck once more, he felt panic set in. Had he actually seen men with gills? "Yes, I did," he attested in no doubt whatsoever. Their gills were as real as the back of his hand. And with that clear comprehension, the implication that his captors would be perfectly at home in the water, struck Joe with force.

"To swim *without* the need to come up for air: they cannot drown!" he realised with fascination. This astounding fact took a while to sink in, but when it finally did, he began to appreciate how marvellous and exciting his young captors in fact were; could they be the perfect creatures? At their disposal, and theirs alone, was the best of both worlds and their possibilities seemed to him limitless. The world truly was their oyster. The cliché rang true for once. And then Joe wondered what the fuss was all about.

In Keegan's world the process of examination was incomplete if one neglected to consider the downside of the matter or question at hand. Proceeding to do just that, he started to question the biology called into play in these circumstances. How did it all work? Those gills, did they obey the call of the sea? What sort of mystical hold did the sea have on these surreal marine humans? How long could they survive in water? Perhaps, that was what the fuss was all about. And, more to the point, for what purpose had they zeroed in on *him* in particular?

It suddenly dawned on Joe that, if anywhere near the truth, his preposterous contemplation about the origins and nature of these young men, these strange marine specimens, had massive implications for the accepted dogma and principles of the creationists. Their foundational beliefs meticulously developed and proliferated over thousands of years would now, emphatically, be in question. Why had something that he now perceived as obvious not occurred to him before?

Disappointed by his mental faculties, Joe felt hugely let down, almost disillusioned. And yet it was inconceivable that he, a steadfast Christian all his life, should lose his faith, indeed his religion. As if on cue, he remembered that: In the beginning, there was darkness and the spirit of God had hovered above the waters. Then God created the Earth. Human beings were the last creatures God made, and they alone, were created in God's image. Joe's faith was grounded on this premise written in the first book of the Bible, Genesis, and it was unimaginable that he should stray from it.

But what did it mean to be created in God's image? Did man physically look like God, a literal interpretation embraced by many, or did the sacred scripture refer instead to His characteristics. "Can it possibly be both of these? Does it matter?" Joe questioned, even though he surely did not know the answer. Could he be parted from a faith of a lifetime - a faith that had given him custody of the Earth? It had seemed beyond possibility, but now he faltered. Bereft of the comfort and unalloyed certainty derived from his faith, Joe was agitated.

"Dear God," he thought, "not in a million years would I have bargained for this quandary."

Being a devout Irish American Catholic boy, he chose not to question his faith – or at least to defer it – and, going easy on himself, he declared his mind too unsettled for serious thought. Even though it was not his preference to delay introspection, he desisted from pondering the question at hand, and allowed his mind to drift instead as it became wildly fanciful and sent him on the path to dreaming about the sea and the creatures in it; the myriad marine life, the fish, the sharks, whales and the dolphins. All of them creatures that to his mind, only ever merely subsisted; creatures endlessly, single-mindedly preoccupied with foraging. They were doomed to subsisting, if not, one would have heard of such a thing as an underwater civilisation.

"No, He will not forsake us," Joe reassured himself, recalling the characteristics he had learned to associate with the Almighty: He was omnipotent, omnipresent and omniscient. "Here is our saving grace," he resolved with relief. Seen in this light, clearly God was prepared. He would have foreseen the rising sea levels and the flooding. If Earth was changing, so would the human species. "He will permit the species to adapt to the times," Joe ascertained, assured that what he had just witnessed in the fish people was God's omniscience at work. God's children would not be left sitting ducks.

He wondered then, how he would feel, if he were like them; like the fish people. The thought brought him back to his own circumstances and the matter of his tag.

"Where exactly have you inserted the tag?" he accusingly asked the man seated beside him.

The look he received was far from encouraging, and for a moment Joe thought he would be ignored.

"It's in your neck, next to one of the carotid arteries. The good thing about that is, if it were triggered, there would be no pain to speak of."

This was delivered in such a matter-of-fact manner, as to make the hair on Joe's nape stand on end. The young man had uttered the words as if he actually believed they would bring comfort. He was courteous, yet determined, and to Joe he seemed immovable, "nothing whatsoever will sway them," he thought helplessly.

"If I am to survive them, I'd better respect that these are no ordinary people," Joe warned himself. Clamouring for hope, "money, I have money," and thinking about his considerable wealth he became excited, nearly convinced that enticement would work. The prospect of even a tiny inducement, he had learned from an early age, worked wonders on people - on swaying them to your side, to conform to your interests.

But wasn't their yacht so much nicer than his? These people could scarcely be motivated by money. And yet he could not dismiss the idea these young men could be bought: "What if the boat is not theirs? What if they are working for someone else?" In that case, perhaps they would be amenable to negotiation. Considering how young they were, spurred him on. A thrill shot down Joe's spine momentarily, kindling an excitement in him. After all, negotiation was his forte.

He stole a look at the man beside him, at his hands, his torso and finally his face, where their glances met. The young man trained his gaze on Joe; his steely glint determined and unwavering, leaving it to his captive to flinch from the confidence and control oozing from him. As Joe's eyes lowered to avoid further scrutiny, he admitted it to himself that he had never seen a blazer, or a pair of trousers fit anyone quite as well. The tailoring was impeccable. The faded, tan corduroy trousers hugged his thighs, betraying tremendous strength. The shoes on his feet were of the finest brown leather and his neatly kept hands betrayed no signs of neglect.

Joe had always prided himself on his skill to tell the sort of man one was, merely by looking at their shoes. The weathered, but highly polished shoes shouted quality and discipline to him, and much more besides. His captor was the epitome of grooming and his clothes screamed refinement and wealth. Those shoes and clothes were made and tailored for him by the best. Only an eye, such as his, would see and appreciate the quality of his clothing. Though appearing nondescript, they were the very best money could buy. To the discerning eye, he would never be just a part of the crowd.

"He is certainly not preoccupied with showing off his wealth, not by his dressing anyway," Joe ascertained. What if he doesn't care for it? What if the young man had dispensed with the care for money? The fact that he had not asked him for any; that there had been no mention whatsoever of a ransom, menacingly stood out. Never before had he met someone who seemed so utterly unaffected by money.

And to reaffirm his assertion, "if he did, he would not be jeopardising his position in this manner, by being a kidnapper." As this insight seemed more likely, Joe squirmed uncomfortably in his seat.

"Abandoning all wealth, but in favour of what?" he desired to know. They must know I am a very rich man. Puzzling over why the subject of money had not been brought up, Joe wondered whether those two could be unaware of his wealth. But that was very unlikely, for they were in possession of his private information, such as how he liked his coffee. Suddenly, having all his money seemed to him petty. Perceiving his fortune in this light was a first for Joe, but it was also the scariest thought he had ever had. His money, it seemed, would not come to his aid this time. "How odd," he thought, feeling bereft and confused. Up until now, his money had secured everything he had set his heart on, whatever his desire had dictated. And in his cynical moments, such as this one, he supposed that it included his wife. "Look at me. If not for the money, what reason would she have to stick with me?" he wondered, recalling the image that met him the last time he stood before a mirror, his twice-broken nose casting a long shadow.

The significance of money, and his life-long pursuit of it, now seemed rather lame under the circumstances. So lame that he laughed bitterly at himself. Even after he had acquired enough of the stuff to last him many lifetimes, he had kept at it. His children, his wonderful children, had in a very real sense grown up without a father. He had hoped that the material distractions money could provide would be enough to make up for his years-long negligence. And yet, he had also been well aware that the novelty and privilege of spending money wore off all too quickly. Certainly, it was no substitute for the void left by one's father, and he himself was an embodiment of the same type of neglect. "Why did I choose my father's path?" he lamented.

Joe knew that financial reward was a powerful motivator. "But these young men have not made any demands for a ransom, which tells me they don't want my money. It would have been so easy if they did, though," he thought regretfully. "And by what means did they come by their fortune?" he wondered. So, if not money, what *was* their motivation? Eliminating financial reward as a motive left Joe baffled.

What he understood quite clearly, however, was that his captors were highly motivated; if nothing else, their ability to totally rearrange his life, to put it politely, was proof of that. And the efficiency with which they had executed their plan took his breath away. His sense of security and well - being had simply disappeared. He had lost all the control he had ever possessed. "What am I to do?" he agonised. "One's fortunes can be so fickle, and, in that sense, they are not so unlike people," he thought, ominously eyeing his captor.

When they arrived at the hotel, his captor's gloved hand passed him a dossier. "In here, you will find your instructions. I would follow them if I were you.

Goodbye," he said crisply, as he handed him his jacket and mobile phone.

The door opened and Joe stepped haltingly out of the limousine. The driver was his interrogator.

20.   *Keegan's dilemma*

Scoping out his surroundings like never before, Joe stealthily walked into the hotel. He entered the open elevator and quickly pushed the button so he could have it all to himself. He was in no mood for sharing. The thought of strangers anywhere near him was terrifying and the jolly elevator tune irritated him to no end. "I will never be my own person," he reckoned. "Those people have seen to it." And how was he to enjoy being driven after this? "You can't trust any of them," he opined with a grunt. Then came the realization that those people were not just 'any of them.' This characterisation was possibly the understatement of the millennium. The thought rankled even more. "My comprehension is flawed," he mumbled. "No one is like them. No one has ever been. Who for example, can claim to be at home in the sea?" he countered.

In his suite, he threw the dossier on the dining table and proceeded to the bedroom. He threw himself on the bed and looked up at the white ceiling. Noticing the recessed lighting, he was reminded of waking up on the yacht.

Experiencing a sudden wave of panic, he sat up abruptly. At a gingerly pace, his right hand examined every inch of skin on his neck. He found his Adam's apple once again and rested his hand there. He pressed his fingers hard into it and, recollecting that the carotid arteries run along the sides of the neck, rather than the middle, ran his fingers along either side of the apple.

"Do I even know what to look for?" he queried. Concluding that he looked for something unusual, something so out of the norm as to defy possibility, he searched a while longer. When he could no longer bear probing, he reached for the phone and called the reception desk to extend his stay by one night. He then placed a call to the pilot of his plane, instructing him to prepare for departure the following day at noon.

"Yes sir, Mr Keegan," the pilot responded with his usual politeness. The reply gave rise in Joe the feeling that he was being mocked, which, in turn, evoked images of his kidnappers. "I will not give them the satisfaction," he declared resolutely, shrugging his shoulders roughly to mask any hint of despair or self-pity.

Intended to encourage, "do people honestly *believe* all that nonsense?" he attacked vehemently. "The planet will take care of itself, as it always has, for millions of years, if not billions." He considered supremely presumptuous those people who actually believed they could take care of the Earth, let alone save it. If asked to describe Earth in one word, he would reply with, "resilient." Anything that old would have learned to adapt to change. "Turn weakness into strength and so on," he argued, applying his own survival technique to the planet. "And why not?" he asked feeling rejuvenated, to the point of pig-headedness. "And let's not forget the matter of God's involvement," he philosophised.

The dossier they had handed to him suddenly came to mind and Joe scrambled off the bed to find it. His obstinacy began to dissipate as he realised that his captors knew everything there was to know about him. And much of it was incriminating. The young men had been extremely thorough in their investigation of his business, his corporation, as well as of his private affairs. They had even provided him with copies of the email correspondence between himself and King Menawa, which he certainly did not write and had no knowledge it existed until now. And he also read the permission he had supposedly written to allow a documentary of his stay to be filmed.

"Those bastards have set out to humiliate me," he thought angrily as their faces flashed again to mind. Then he remembered the notes he had written down when he read the article that led him to hire Oliver, his PR guy.

"No!" He was horrified. "It can't be." Yet, upon reflection, it seemed to add up. Their faces were in fact *not* real – they wore masks! While their eyes had betrayed passion, none had been etched on their faces. Right from the start, Joe had sensed something very peculiar, discordant, and he now realised that his first impulse had been the right one: the young men wore very sophisticated, cinema-quality masks.

It dawned once again on Joe, how intimately his detainers seemed to know him. They had adroitly responded to his challenging outbursts by showing him the footage that immediately shut him up. So well prepared were they, that, at every step, they had incapacitated him. "They can read me like an open book!" he concluded angrily. At the top of his thoughts now lay the realisation that he could easily be murdered. They had told him as much.

Fathoming death was unfamiliar to Joe, sobering in the most morbid, deflating way. In the past he kept the notion of it at arm's length. Even the preparation of his will had not invoked thoughts of his own mortality. He had thought the act purely a matter of practicality, a bit of bureaucracy on his part and a necessity for people like him. Now that death loomed large, perhaps he might be inclined to change his will.

Shifting focus, Joe reached for the phone and dialled his publicist's number from memory. Frightened his mind might go to pot he routinely committed telephone numbers to memory, as part of the regimen to exercise his brain. "Better get this out of the way," he thought, unable to suppress a sense of resignation and sadness.

"Hello, Christine, it's Joe. I'd like you to arrange a press conference for precisely ten o'clock tomorrow morning. Invite the usual suspects." He paused for her response and answered, "Yes, here at the hotel." After a short pause: "Oh, as for the subject, let's just leave that open for now," he said wryly.

Knowing he would not relish her reaction if she were informed of his purpose, he decided not to say a word. She would be at a complete loss, but only for an instant, before her sharp mind pointed out all the risk factors and the evidence weighed against him. She would inevitably declare his decision foolhardy, tantamount to self-sacrifice. Having a sixth sense for the uncanny, she would detect that something was amiss. Feeling the way he did, he was quite certain further discourse would ultimately leave him unhinged and possibly lead him to reveal his secret. Recollecting Christine's favourite rejoinder: "You pay me a lot of money, the least I can do is talk straight and keep you out of trouble."

Therefore, he curtly responded, "wait for the surprise."

"Come on Joe!" she protested. "In my line of work, surprises rarely do the trick."

Though he agreed with her wholeheartedly, he could not say so. Instead, he slowly put the phone back. Why was he in all this trouble? Why was he being punished for merely adopting innovation and putting it to good use for his business as well as for society at large? Oil was not a luxury, but rather a need. Out of necessity, companies like his were forced to innovate, to adopt new technology in order to get at the oil that would otherwise be beyond reach. He remembered the day the idea was presented to him rather clearly. As he had listened to the ideas man, introduced to him by the chief engineer of Keegan Oil, he had kept thinking: "There is a catch here somewhere, surely." But the case presented to him had been clear, straightforward and compelling. The man was in possession of the knowledge required to wash oil out of sand. It was an incredible notion. And this sand lay in Canada, their peaceful neighbour to the North. When convinced, he had left it to his chief engineer to iron out the details while he travelled to Alberta to formally acquire his portion of the pie. The rest, as the saying goes, was water under the bridge.

"Why didn't I organise some security?" he ruminated bitterly while replaying the events of the previous evening in his head. He had received the call to go down at seven. Five minutes later, or thereabouts, he slipped into that limo and they sped off. When they finally stopped, far from arriving at his destination, as he had expected, he got the surprise of his life. He could scarcely believe how surreal his life had become since that moment.

21. *The press conference*

Joe woke up at five thirty on the day of the press conference. Seeking reassurance about his whereabouts, he quickly scanned the room. Satisfied, he sighed with relief and glanced at the heavy curtains covering the windows. "If it was a bright and sunny morning, those curtains would certainly keep the light out." Expecting sunshine, much less daylight, this early on a winter's day, he realised, was wistful.

After a long, soul-searching night replaying petrifying themes over and over again in his restless mind, he was surprised he had slept at all. The memory of his phone call home now brought a smile to his sleepy face. Yes, he had face timed his family. Realising, it was their father calling his daughters had jostled excitedly for his attention as their chirpy voices had fought to be heard above those of the others. Coming at last to his rescue, his wife took the phone from the girls and had spoken to him while their daughters calmed down. When she asked about the dinner party, he had said: "There were no surprises. It was completely uneventful, just as I had expected," and he had laughed loudly. In supposed collusion with her husband, Marjorie had laughed along, but on this occasion, she could be forgiven for misunderstanding his laughter altogether. Asking about his plans while in Canada, Joe fell silent, all of a sudden unsure how to cope with her questioning. Thinking about the press conference, he had revealed that he was still in Washington D.C. "I will leave tomorrow at noon. Can I speak to the kids now, honey?"

In the hour he spent talking in turn to each of his children, under the pretext that nothing had happened to him, he had masked his anxiety well. Listening intently to their animated chatter, Joe had felt uplifted and, for a fleeting moment, free of worry. Seeing his thriving and content family reinforced his decision to keep Marjorie in the dark.

Niles had retained his place on the ski team. "I made it again this year, Dad." On his end of the line, Joe heard the pride in his young son's voice. Though enthusiastic, his response was tinged with shame; he had not been to any of his son's skiing competitions. Acutely aware, his son was gracious enough to gloss over the matter. Instead, Niles talked animatedly about the latest advances in skiing technology and his desire to buy a particular brand of skis. "They are fairly expensive, Dad. Do you think I can get an early Christmas present?" he cajoled mildly. Joe had agreed eagerly. Of his possessions and material things he gave willingly to his family, but rarely of himself.

"I was a bit afraid, you know, Daddy. But Miss Olga said to focus on her all the time and follow her lead. And that's what I did. It went great!" Lily had excitedly recounted her latest performance of ballet. Her excitement was contagious, and he had wanted to hear more. With patience he had listened to her describe the costume she had worn in detail.

Violet gave an account of the birthday party she had attended the day before. "I was allowed to stay later than the others coz she's my best friend. Mommy picked me up after seven," she said with heartfelt gratitude. The mention of seven cut through his pretence for a moment, "it was at seven o'clock I got into that car," he recalled, but quickly noted that Violet spoke about Mountain Time.

Rosie had begged him to ask her mother to let her go to Denver with her friends, without parental supervision, and he had promised he would try, even though the idea frightened him. Just as he was about to plead his daughter's case, his wife tensely interrupted, "totally out of the question."

After bidding them goodnight, he had found that he missed them all desperately. They were his flesh and blood. At present, he longed for them in a manner unknown to him. "If only I could see them," he cried out in torment. Swearing violently under his breath, "I will not rest until those two and their accomplices are properly dealt with. Unless they kill me first." And if they succeeded, he supposed that would be the end of that. "No," he thought, "if they kill me first, then they will have won. And I just cannot allow that to happen." The prospect of a premature demise was so infuriating that his nostrils flared as his hands clenched tightly into fists. To have life was everything, for without it, there was nothing left. There was no will left with which to accomplish anything. Relieved of life, one was left pitifully wanting.

"Am I as good as gone? Going once, going twice and finally gone: I am at the going phase for sure, the pendulum has begun its swing..." though undecided as to whether he was at the first or the second stage.

Joe resolved to calm himself, and to bide his time. He would play along and act obedient, all the while gathering intelligence to lay a fine plan, and when the time came – for it would sooner or later surely come – he would seize his chance. If granted a full year at the reservation, as told, that would be more than enough time.

When the duration of his stay at the reservation finally registered, Joe felt a panic rise. How could he have forgotten? He had blithely overlooked the internal reports on environmental impact, the ones he and his management team had confidently dismissed as inconsequential. The information of widespread toxins polluting the reservation especially its river – the only source of drinking water – was all of a sudden, incredibly consequential. Separating oil from sand was technically more involved than he had been led to believe; the process produced a significant amount of chemical waste. And this waste was proving impossible to contain. "But what venture is without challenge?" he had protested at the time.

...

By no means subdued, at precisely ten o'clock, Joe Keegan entered the conference room. Purposefully trotting up the steps to the podium, he felt that his sense of self-preservation was now stronger than it had ever been. At the podium he flashed his dazzling white smile at the women and men of the media. "Good morning ladies and gentlemen of the press," he said, his easy charm and winsome smile on full display. His eyes skimmed across the row of reporters sitting at the front of the room, slowly moved through the middle ranks before proceeding to the back of the room along the wall, where the photographers were assembled, cameras at the ready.

Peter lifted his imposing digital camera to take shots of the man on the podium. When he took a pause and lowered his arms, Joe's gaze rested squarely on him. He kept his own eyes steady and on point, but Joe's face betrayed no recognition; his gaze was met as that of a stranger. And that was as he had expected.

Hastily substituting the friendly, affable Joe with the no-nonsense chief executive who no longer beamed, Mr Keegan commenced his briefing: "By now I am sure you've all heard all sorts of speculations on our activities in Alberta. In the past, I have given repeated assurance that our extraction activities are 100% compliant with the relevant environmental regulations. Now, to put my money where my mouth is, in order to once and for all demonstrate my good faith and to silence the detractors, I hereby announce that, upon the invitation of King Menawa, I am moving to Alberta to live on the Potowak Reservation."

Listening to Joe utter the very words he himself had used to express his indignation with him, irritated Peter terribly. It was as though Keegan was mocking him.

"I have invited our friends from the Blue Green Planet Television Network to document every aspect of my stay on the reservation. The documentary will be aired on their public television station over the course of the year. To be clear, the purpose of my visit is to establish that we are, and always will remain true to protecting the environment and the communities that depend on it. Our activities in the oil sands are safe and clean. Keegan Oil has always adhered strictly and diligently to existing environmental laws and regulations that are designed to protect our planet. With that in mind, I look forward to spending the coming year in Alberta and will enjoy residing downriver from the oil sands, on the banks of the beautiful Seno River. Thank you for your considerate attention."

Joe resisted the urge to speak longer; it was not necessary for this particular purpose. In any case, experience had taught him that keeping it short, sweet and to the point was usually the best approach. Only fools enjoyed listening to themselves!

Peter wondered about the sort of images the word "downriver" conjured up for Mr Keegan. Such images would, of course, be linked to individual experience. For some, a river was a place to row one's boat gently downstream, while blissfully leaving the worries and cares of the day, indeed of life, far behind. While on the river to be entertained, by the spectacle of fish jumping out to the surface to snatch a tempting morsel. For others, the riverbank was a pristine location for a picnic, from which to watch the river steadily flow by and, on happy occasion, to witness a family of ducks, glide by effortlessly. Without question the age-old favourite for countless, was perhaps a chilly, but invigorating dip in the river on a hot summer's day.

These romantic images, anchored in a melodramatic comprehension of nature unhinged from reality, were distinctly foreign to Peter. The images that cropped up in his mind exposed his special vulnerability. "That man has no, no …" the word he grappled for was obscured by the alarming images of his own very real downriver ordeal. He struggled to dispel the sinister images, but they fastened to him and undermined his resolve to be unaffected. The undeniable tension he suddenly encountered, allowed fear and apprehension to firmly take hold. Whereas in the past, the downriver misadventure had given him strength and a sense of purpose, taken thus by surprise, it had brought his guard down.

He was grasping for control when the word he searched vainly for finally came to mind. "Scruples. Yes, that's it! That's it exactly," he thought. "The man has no scruples! He's immoral, utterly immune to pangs of conscience." The fear of where his loss of control might lead further undermined his will.

His agitation grew and, despite his desperate efforts to resist, in the ensuing, excruciating moments, Peter's physiology sealed off his lungs. Even though he was nowhere near the ocean, his gills were activated! In Peter's young life, extreme agitation had always led to this type of malfunction of his respiratory organs. In order to counter it, he and his siblings had learned and practiced enormous self-restraint. It was not merely for the purpose of self-discipline; it was a simple matter of survival. Incipient species were not immune to transitioning issues, as they were understood to be, and this particular attribute, was a veritable Achille's heel for him and his siblings. Well, this and the cleft palates they had been born with, which, mercifully, had been relatively easy fixes.

Though Peter worked frantically to restore lung function, his efforts were in vain; he was incapable of gasping for air.

22. The dead zone

His eyelids grew heavy and began to droop. The room reeled as the flashing lights from the cameras around him began to dim. His strength fading fast now, his faculties, one after the other, were shutting down.

"Not now, not here," his overcome mind begged. His grip on the camera loosened and his hands fell limply to his side. His body leaden and buckling, he grappled for the wall behind. He was suffocating ... powerless.

Images from a similar calamity shot unremittingly through his panic-filled mind, compelling him to relive the terrifying downriver mishap. Although just as insidious, it was different from the painful, bodily malfunction he was now in the grip of in one crucial respect: it happened underwater. The incident, if ever he had had the slightest doubt, revealed the depravity of the human race and made plain to him the self-destructive path humans had chosen ... a path that mocked their very existence.

On that day, not unlike any one of the thousand other days, he dove into the ocean with great zeal, not a care in the world, and completely in his element. Just before he hit the water, he blinked purposefully to activate his nictitating membranes. When he opened his shielded eyes deep in the water, his vision was perfect. He had swallowed a mouthful of water to kick-start his aquatic respiration and seawater had tingled its way into his gills in the odd manner to which he was accustomed. He had continued to dive, intent on reaching a great depth.

Seconds later, he had innately sensed the presence of Alex gliding beside him, and without looking he had known his brother's exact orientation. In more ways than one, water was his medium for surviving the vast oceanic environment. Minute vibrations travelling through the water, were processed by his body into valuable information, to guide and to protect. He was equipped with a most precious sensory mechanism called a lateral line, which run along his sides comprising mechanoreceptors that transduced and interpreted the vibrations created by virtually any movement in the water. Yes, there was more to a fish than met the eye. As a result, he had known precisely how fast his brother swam and the direction in which he was headed. He perceived intuitively, too, the orientation of other creatures in the vicinity. On that particular day, myriad jellyfish had populated his part of the ocean.

He revelled in his receptor trait for it enabled him to school with his siblings. He considered his lateral line amazing. His poor father was still perplexed by it, while his mother had unparalleled appreciation for the safety it afforded them. In any case, Peter understood that his parent's discernment could not possibly match his own.

He had taken care to explain to them the process and function of his inborn, aquatic respiration, comparing it to a garden fountain's first spouting after a long winter fallow. To begin with, the fountain's operation was irregular, the initial discharge short, sputtering and weak. The second rush of water arrived stronger and more rhythmic than the first, but it too was short-lived. Usually, the fountain's third attempt finally produced a steady, unbroken flow.

In a manner similar, with his lungs tightly sealed, his gills initially spewed and sputtered until making the transition and, from then on, it was effortless respiration, so to speak. The transformation thus complete, he and his brother and sister were as comfortable in the water as on land. Submerged in seawater, they became fish, except no ordinary fish – one with gills as well as lungs! Much like the renowned lungfish that experts in evolutionary biology have identified as Homo sapiens' pelagic ancestor. In the first trimester of pregnancy, human embryos have gills.

In Peter and his siblings, the gills were re-selected. The regression triggered by the lead poisoning endured by five generations of their ancestors at the Broken Hill lead and zinc mine. Eventually, the poisoning had overpowered and transmuted the DNA that normally supressed full-blown gill development in modern humans. The same DNA that ensured coalescence during embryonic development of the five facial lobes, transforming the fish visage into what we recognise as the human face. Gills, the cleft palate and nictitating eye membranes were, thus, remnant genes stemming from our time at sea.

He had drawn more water into his gills, the process now well underway and, yet, he felt gradually more light-headed. Again and again he had filled his gills to capacity and fought to absorb the oxygen in it, each time with greater volumes of seawater. But something was terribly amiss; there was no relief. Feeling faint despite several more mouthfuls, panic set in. Frantically inhaling gulps, Peter had gone rigid with fear. He could not fathom what was happening to him. His body had jerked and convulsed uncontrollably until it had at last dawned on him that he was suffocating. At the same time, his reading on Alex's movement was strange and began to break up; it was not at all what he was used to. Peter's distress surged when he realised that Alex, like him, must be convulsing from the lack of oxygen: "we are both dying." Fear spread unchecked inside him as he wondered, "but, where is Katfish?"

"I am too young to die," he had shuddered. The memory of his mother's apprehensive demeanour, which she miserably failed to mask when she bade them goodbye before a dive, made him cry out: "She won't survive her children dying at seventeen!" As darkness enveloped him, he could no longer sense Alex.

There in the Gulf of Mexico, where the Mississippi flowed unimpeded for miles and miles into the sea, Peter lay dying, trapped in waters that arrived from far and near, from mountain and plain; incalculable quantities poisoned as a result of human beings' insatiable quest for money.

On a clear day, this majestic river was visible from space as a dark ribbon of ink coursing far out into the Gulf, its might steadily diluted. Silt and toxins from the American hinterland – as well as nitrate-rich chemical fertiliser – were carried forth without pause or interruption. Thus let loose, the nitrates drove unnaturally high levels of toxic algae growth. As the algae bloom expired, it sucked oxygen from the water, creating dead zones. Had he been able to dive deeper, Peter would have encountered evidence of the malicious effect spread out on the seabed - pallid skeletons, empty shells and other fragments of once-living aquatic organisms. This was the dreaded dead zone of the Gulf of Mexico, a foreboding and barren expanse of ocean; an ecosystem fit only for the resilient jellyfish, which were assuming immense proportions and growing exceptionally in number.

At the critical moment, Kat had arrived seemingly from nowhere to rescue her brothers. She had been quick to discern the eeriness of the water, the multitude of abnormally large jellyfish, and a marine space devoid of any other life - form. Of the siblings, only Kat had been wise to the fact that jellyfish lived on negligible amounts of oxygen. She had swum to the surface and filled her lungs to capacity before diving in search of her brothers. Then, following the discordance of their convulsive vibrations, she had reached them just before they passed out.

***

In a semi-conscious state, propped up by the wall in the back of the pressroom, Peter's body relaxed and, nature being wilful, biologic instinct kicked in and forced open his sealed lungs. He jerked upright and coughed vigorously.

As oxygen rushed into his lungs, the ringing in his head subsided. "That's better...not a moment too soon," a wave of relief washed over Peter. As his senses and faculties were gradually restored, Joe Keegan's booming voice reverberated once more in his ears. Taking another precious breath, he looked sidelong around the room still chockfull of members of the press. But no one minded him...not a soul had paid any heed to his sudden, respiratory seizure. He clutched the camera strap around his neck with gratitude and smiled self-consciously.

How did it happen? Why now? Perhaps exposing his secret to Joe Keegan had made him vulnerable at some subliminal level, and caused him to drop his guard, precipitating the malfunction. He resolved there and then that this would never happen again.

A fifty-something journalist in a crumpled brown jacket raised his hand and rose from his chair. "Mr Caine from the Herald Tribune," he pronounced. "Sounds like quite the drastic decision for you, Mr Keegan. I must say you've taken a lot of people by surprise. So much so that I cannot help but conclude this decision is not entirely your own. Care to comment on who might be leaning on you, sir?"

Joe was unfazed; he looked pensive for a moment, as if troubled, but then responded serenely: "No decision, no issue is drastic when it comes to protecting my interests, and that is exactly what I am doing here. Since my interests are intrinsically linked to society at large, I am convinced, now more than ever, that we, fellow citizens of this solitary planet, must pull together."

Joe knew his stage and audience really well; he was in his element. His response was befitting any captain of industry. And this particular captain was eloquent and steady, even when lying through his teeth.

Kenny Horan, senior production executive from the Green Blue Planet Media Corporation, cleared his throat and thanked Joe for giving his company the opportunity to document his stay. "How will you cope with the reportedly high levels of contamination at the reservation, Mr Keegan?" he asked.

Peter was delighted by the man's question. "Why aren't more of them as curious and direct?"

For an instant, Joe froze. "It's really my pleasure, Kenny, to have you on board for this mission. Keegan Oil believes in complete transparency and this endeavour will prove that we have nothing to hide, nothing whatsoever. And as for myself, I have nothing to fear. In fact, I can't wait to get on the plane."

"Let the battle begin," Peter declared calmly in mind, "and if there is any justice at all, my side will prevail." As expected, Joe's performance was polished, "the man still has it in him."

It wasn't lost on Peter that, for the most part, the people whose mandate was to seek the truth, the journalists gathered here, had willingly permitted the lying and subterfuge. This was far more dispiriting. Their line of questioning was pathetic; they seemed either unwilling to, or incapable of piercing the layers of deceit. Why on earth did they not pose the difficult, but truly obvious and important questions? Questions to have revealed the corruption and to have held Keegan and his company to account. He and Alex had handed Joe Keegan to the press on a silver platter. For instance, why were they not interested in the disappearance of the doctor who had treated the cancer patients on the reservation? What about the reports that Keegan Oil had advanced a large sum to the Chief Officer of the Safety Board?

To put it mildly, as ostensible truth seekers this group of journalists proved disappointing. The accomplished oil executive holding forth today was without question a poised, charming man, skilled at artful communication. With so much at stake, however, one could be forgiven for expecting that charm would not obscure or render meaningless the suffering of thousands of people caused by this man … or the countless other lives that still hung in the balance.

Peter reflected gravely on the commission he and his siblings had taken on, their quest for justice in a wicked world, a world that shuns justice. Their endeavour was perilous, but what choice did they have? While they were being pushed to the very edge of existence and the poisoning of our planet continued unabated, much of the world remained complacent and indifferent. How would they ever manage to put things right?

His near-death experience in the Gulf so clear in his mind as if it happened only yesterday, Peter harshly conceded, "though I was just a kid then, I should have known." Often now, when on land, he was filled with panic at the mere thought, "if a dead zone at sea, why not here on terra firma?" Haunted by the prospect of walking blindly into a vacuum, within he forcefully demanded: "What good is all the money in the world, if one cannot breathe?"

Printed in Great Britain
by Amazon

60966371R00132